AN ORMAN'S REVENGE

Part of the Truson S.E.T. Series

DOMINIQUE GIBSON

ISBN: 13-978-1-7345706-4-9 (Hardcover)
ISBN: 13-978-1-7345706-6-3 (Paperback)

Dedication

I would like to dedicate this book to my mother who has always supported me. To Judy Roth, who turned this ugly duckling into a beautiful swan and to my boyfriend. Thank you for your support in this journey.

Sign up for my newsletter!

Do you want to keep up with the latest updates, articles and more? Sign up for my monthly newsletter on my website at dominiquegibsonauthor.com or you can catch me on Facebook and Twitter to learn more. Hope to see you again real soon.

www.dominiquegibsonauthor.com.

List of terms for the **Truson S.E.T series**:

Animan three-hundred: A potion that mixes dead human and animal DNA in order to create hybrids. In this case, the Animan three-hundred was used to create Ormans.

Ormans: A race of half-human, half-orcas that lives on the island of Truson.

Island of Truson: An island that's isolated from the rest of the world that was created by Benjamin Truson and Courtney Madison for a safe hiding place for the Ormans and other species to live on after the U.S. government declared it was no longer safe to keep them scattered throughout the world.

Binosil: A liquid medicine used to stop the human-animal transformation whenever it is too dangerous for a human to transfer into their animal form.

Alter Ego: The animal side of the human species that's rises to the surface every twelve hours (normally at night). The only exception would be if the dead human was injected with the Animan three-hundred for the first twenty-four to forty-eight hours.

Truson Super Elite Team: A bunch of half-human, half-animal hybrids who are sworn to protect humans from criminals both on land and water.

Book of Truson: A manual that contains specific information about how the Truson S.E.T. was born, starting from ancient Egypt until the present day in addition to the laws of Truson to keep the Truson S.E.T's powers from spinning out of control.

The Transforments: A group of orcas that was once created by Samuel Holifield as a way to retaliate revenge on the Truson S.E.T. after being kicked out of the group for killing innocent humans and Ormans combined.

CHAPTER ONE

Ford Mayfield sat back in his chair and crossed his legs. Staring at the redheaded beauty lying a few inches away, he tapped his foot every so often to keep his feet from falling asleep. He scoffed, unable to believe that Dr. Courtney Madison, a pharmacologist capable of bringing dead humans back to life as shapeshifters, persuaded him to train the woman who mysteriously washed up along the shores of Truson.

His island.

She knew how he felt about bringing a new woman into his daily activities, especially since it was getting close to the anniversary of his wife's death.

There were many things he had planned for the day—one of them involved being at the Truson School for Shapeshifters, training a new set of shapeshifters who had already gone through the process of the Animan Three-Hundred and were now ready to become better Ormans. Even though it was summer on the island of Truson, the school held classes all year round due to the painful transformation of the Animan Three-Hundred.

If he didn't get back to his students soon, disaster would strike. Ford shook his head. All he needed was for one Orman to escape the island and attack anyone who got in the way.

And the secret society they worked so hard to create would be destroyed…

The woman shifted her weight in the bed. The chains jingled with every movement she made. Poor girl. Ford got up from his chair and inched closer. His mind replayed what happened to him when he arrived on the island while he took a couple more steps, staring at the purple and blue bruises the chains left behind.

Should I release her? He thought. *She seems to be in a lot of pain.* He cringed. Why did the corporal punishment of an Orman have to be so brutal?

Before he found the answer to his question, the woman jolted up from the bed, and Ford backed away. The chains held her from escaping her bed, causing her to sit in an upright position. Ford watched the woman stare at the wall before she let out a blood-curdling scream.

Taking a couple of breaths, he tried to remember what the woman had gone through before she was chained up like an animal. After being given the scare of his life, Ford somehow managed to push himself off the wall and comfort her as best he could.

"It's okay. I know it hurts, but it will pass. I promise," he said. Ford wrapped his arms around her, the chains cutting into his skin like ice. It didn't help that the woman struggled out of his grasp, desperately seeking a way out of the chains that shackled her. *How long is this going to take?*

The woman stopped screaming and collapsed on the bed. He panicked. He knew the Animan Three-Hundred was only used on dead humans. If the woman was hollering, it could mean one thing.

The Animan Three-Hundred was working.

Dr. Madison's words fluttered to his mind. He'd asked her why she decided to investigate Mandy's dead body after finding her washed up off the shores of Truson which had only been a couple of hours ago.

"You have to believe me when I say it will be worth it."

"Worth it how?" Ford had asked.

"Let's just say she is connected to someone you've wanted to see disappear for years."

Ford massaged his chin. The only person he wanted to see dead was the one person who was responsible for his wife's death.

"So, you got a lead on who killed my wife?"

Dr. Madison had stopped typing on her computer and spun around.

"Boss, I really can't give you any details about this right now. I'm still working on the connection, but I will let you know when I receive more information. I just want to be sure everything is accurate, okay?"

Ford had wanted to protest but decided to drop the subject.

The woman's eyes opened and stared at the ceiling. Something stirred inside him. He'd seen plenty of women with green eyes but never as vibrant as what he was staring at right now. They were marvelous, mysterious…

Deadly.

Her eyes changed from sparkling light green to a dazzling aquamarine. She only held the appearance for a few moments before it disappeared and the marvelous light green eyes that stirred his emotions came back again. Her eyes turned to Ford.

He straightened himself up and got his emotions in check while greeting the woman with a smile.

"Did you get a good night's rest?" he asked. It was only after he said it, he realized how much of a mistake he'd made when it came to that question. "Sorry, I didn't mean to be so insensitive."

The woman licked her lips and swallowed.

"Where…am…I? The…lights…too…bright…"

Ford went over to the other side of the room and adjusted the lighting until it became nothing more than the reflection of a brightly lit candle surrounding the place.

"Better?"

She nodded.

Ford grabbed one of the rollaway chairs near the desk on the right side of the room. He rolled the chair to the woman's bed and sat down.

"How are you feeling?" he asked, knowing what the obvious answer was going to be, but he needed some information to report back to Dr. Madison.

"My head…my legs…burning," she said.

"The chains are cutting off your circulation." Ford grabbed the lock from one of her legs and held it in his palm. A spark of flame burst through the middle of his hand until he was able to unlock it and set her legs free.

Once that was accomplished, he set the rest of the locks free, and all of the chains collapsed on the floor.

The woman wiggled her toes then her fingers. She was probably stiff as a board, unaware she had been chained up for the last forty-eight hours.

"Thank…you," she said. She lifted her head, but it flopped back down on the pillow. "So…thirsty…"

Ford searched for anything the doctor might have left behind for her. Nothing. No cups, no water, no ice cubes, not even something to make her feel comfortable. What was Dr. Madison thinking?

She was transformed once upon a time, she should have known what a dead human went through after a transformation like this. He buried his thoughts. There was no time for anger and resentment. He needed to ask her questions about her family.

"I know you're thirsty right now, but I need to ask some questions first." He paused. When the woman didn't respond to his request, he continued.

"Do you know who you are?" Ford wanted to punch himself. He quickly regained his composure and rephrased the question. "Do you remember your name?"

The woman's eyes drifted to his face.

Ford felt his palms getting sweaty. Blood rushed through his veins. Something was tugging inside his body.

It couldn't be…

"No," she finally said. Her throat moved." Don't remember…my…name. Don't…remember anything."

"So, you don't remember how you got here?"

"No."

Amnesia? It was possible. Ford replayed the conversation in his head.

"How did…I…get here?" she asked.

There was no way to soften the blow. Eventually, she was going to learn the truth about who she was and how she got here in the first place. Since Dr. Madison failed at making her feel like a guest on the island, he had to make sure she wouldn't escape.

"You suffered injuries from a car accident a few miles away. It was pretty bad. I don't know how it happened, but your car ended up in the water. Your body was found washed up on this island." She lifted her brow.

"Island?"

"Yes," Ford replied. "We call this the island of Truson. A lot of people have trouble finding it because it's so far away from every island and country on Earth." Silence. Ford thought about what he said and hoped he was doing the right thing. He didn't want to give too much information so soon. The woman needed to adjust to her surroundings.

And he needed to adjust his alter ego who wouldn't stop tugging at him to come out and play…

"From every island on Earth?" The woman grimaced.

"Yes," he said. "Are your arms and legs feeling better?" Ford watched as the woman moved her toes and fingers—a good sign her feet hadn't been entirely numb.

"Ok, since we're making progress on your recovery, why don't we try walking to the nearest fountain for some water?" She had to be dying of thirst. He was quite thirsty himself. He needed to replenish himself after spending twenty-four hours with someone he didn't know.

Despite her beauty, after what happened to his wife ten years ago, he swore he would never love a woman again. No other woman was ever going to compare to Roxanne Gene Mayfield.

No one.

"Need…water," she said. The woman slid her right leg off the bed and hung it there much to Ford's dismay. He couldn't help but stare at her luscious legs and thought about how much he wanted to—what? Kiss them? There was no way possible. Sure, he liked the way they looked, but that didn't mean he wanted to kiss them.

What the hell was wrong with him?

The woman slid her other leg down on the floor. Ford grabbed her by her waist, ready to support her if she were to fall once she landed. Fortunately, she was able to balance herself without his help.

"Ready?" he asked.

She nodded.

The walk started out slow. The woman took careful steps following Ford's lead.

"Thank you…for helping me."

Ford managed a smile.

"You're welcome." *The woman seems nice,* Ford thought. As they passed the beautiful paintings and sculptures along the walls and floor of the Truson Headquarters, he couldn't help but sneak glances at her physique—Something he'd never done with the other women he dated after losing Roxanne.

Ford found it to be distracting. Here he was trying to help the woman based on a favor for the pharmacologist who gave him a second chance in life, and all he could think about was the shape of her breasts and how they reminded him of his past. He had slept with countless women since Roxanne's death, but the shape of her breasts wasn't like anything he'd ever seen before.

Hers were round and pump and ready to pop out at any minute.

His alter ego tugged at him once again. It wanted to come out and enjoy the company before him. He could feel his powers burning.

No, not now. The last thing Ford needed was to change into his alter ego in front of her. If he were to evolve into an orca now, the woman would inevitably run in the other direction.

He couldn't let that happen.

"What's your…name?" Ford heard her ask. His mind focused on controlling his alter ego again as it got stronger and more aggressive, but luckily, he was able to fight it off.

"My name's Ford." Ford studied her as she stared at the floor.

Moisture formed around her eyes before she finally met his gaze.

"I'm so…sorry. I wish I…could tell you…my name but I…I don't know…what my name is." She stopped when Ford put his hands up.

"It's okay. I know you don't remember. If it helps, I can tell you your name," Ford said.

She paused before taking her first finger and thumb of her right hand and applying it to her index finger of her left. *Weird* Ford thought. It was only when the woman moved her hands that Ford saw an imprint of a ring and thought back to his conversation with Dr. Madison.

He felt a little betrayed because she hadn't mentioned anything to him about the woman possibly being married to someone who he could only assume was dangerous to both humans and orcas.

"Hello, can you…hear me?" she asked.

His mind retreated back to her. Dammit, why couldn't he concentrate?

"I'm sorry, what was the question again?"

She stiffened. "What's my name?"

"Yes, of course," he said. "Your name is Mandy Stevenson. It's what was on your state ID when we found your purse in the car."

"Do you still have it?" she asked. She cocked her head to the side and waited for Ford's response.

"No. Dr. Madison has all of your belongings in a locked cabinet on the third floor of this building. We'll probably make a tour around the building later." Ford pressed the button. "Water?"

"I can get it myself." Mandy shoved his hand away and bent over. Her hair fell over her face while she savored the liquid flowing down her mouth. The cooling sensation lifted some of the pain edged in her throat. Once she was done, she flipped her hair back and straightened her shoulders.

Ford groaned as the smell of mango and strawberries invaded his nostrils.

"I think it's time I sent you back to your room." He wanted to get as far away from her as possible. He didn't like the sensations flooding through his body after watching her perform. He felt his abdomen tingle with excitement when she stared at him.

"Why? Is there something wrong?" she asked.

Yes, my alter ego won't shut up, my body feels like it's about to explode, and I really don't have time to explain any of this to you.

Ford shrugged. "I know you're probably tired from today's events. I think you should go back and lie down for a while."

Mandy raised a brow. "If I didn't know any better, I would say you were trying to get rid of me."
Ford took his fingers and squeezed his forehead.

"I'm not trying to get rid of you. You've had a long day. The transformation is a very long and exhausting process—"

"—Transformation? What do you mean by that?" she interrupted.

Damn. Ford wanted to take things slow when it came to this situation, but his alter ego was screaming to get out. He needed Mandy to cooperate and not ask any questions he couldn't answer at the moment.

"It's when you transform from one thing to another."

"I know what the word means, I'm not illiterate. I'm asking what it means when it comes to me?"

She's a feisty one. Ford's insides stirred again. He tried to think of ways he could explain it but felt like he was wasting his time. Why couldn't he just get the information he wanted and go back to the life he'd had before? Ford grunted. Considering the condition, there was no way she was going to provide the answers he desperately needed.

There had to be more to the story than Dr. Madison had led on.

"It means you are no longer one hundred percent human. You died in the accident. You're an Orman now."

***

No longer a hundred percent human? An Orman? Mandy laughed. Was this man serious? Of course, she was human. She had two arms, two legs and had declared herself lucky to be alive after finding out she had survived what sounded like a very horrific car accident. Where did this man come from, a psych ward? Mandy wiped away her tears of laughter as Ford gave her a stern look, one that screamed he wasn't too happy about her reaction to the situation.

"What's so funny?" he asked.

"Oh c'mon, do you honestly expect me to believe I'm not human and I'm an Ormu or whatever it is you called it?" Mandy wiped the rest of her tears and exhaled.

"I'm telling the truth, Mandy. You are somewhat still human but not like you used to be. You're different now," he said. Ford stepped closer to her. "Don't you feel something tugging at you to come out?"

Mandy let the words sink in. She did feel a little funny. There was something…different about her.

"It's like you have another person inside trying to get out. It wants to be free to explore the environment to see if you are in any sort of danger. It's part of who you are now."

Mandy took a couple of steps back from him. She had to admit this man, whoever he was, did something to her she'd never experienced before. Her heart raced, and her knees buckled whenever he was close to her.

Not good.

"Mandy?"

Mandy drew her attention back to him. "No, I don't feel anything," she lied. She did feel something pulling her in but decided she needed to figure out what it was on her own. Though he had been kind enough to unlock her from those horrid chains that blocked off her circulation, something deep inside told her not to trust him. Could Ford have been right about her? Was she only half-human?

"So, you don't feel anything?" He stepped closer. "You don't feel the sensation of powers running through your veins? The blood rush you get when your other form starts taking over?" Ford took a few more steps toward her. "You mean to tell me you don't feel any of those things?"

She stirred. The contact was way too close for comfort. As they continued to gaze at each other, she realized what Ford meant when it came to that weird feeling she got every time he was near her.

Something nuzzled inside her, wanting to be free. Free from what? She wasn't sure. Maybe it was time to go back to bed. It would give her the opportunity to get away from the man who looked hell-bent on kissing her. Mandy tried to back away from him, but a strange pain took over her legs.

"What's wrong? What's happening?" Ford asked.

Mandy put her hands on her legs and felt the pain and tingling associated with it.

When Ford touched her back, shots of electricity flung through his skin, causing him to step back.

"My legs…my legs hurt really bad. I think I need to go see a doctor!" Mandy's legs were stuck like glue as she collapsed on the floor.

***

Ford watched her legs transform into one large flipper. It wasn't a good sign. She was converting into an orca, and if he didn't react quickly, her weight would be too heavy to hold on his own.

He needed to get her out of here—fast!

Ford wasted little time wrapping his arms around Mandy as she lay there, becoming a prisoner to her own alter ego. He carried her in his arms and searched for the nearest exit to the island. He ran with her through a maze of dimly lit hallways and huge aquariums big enough to fit at least three orcas. Ford started to rethink his plan.

If he was able to access the laboratory with a key card, he could put Mandy in there for the time being until she was able to transform herself back into human form. Ford thought hard about where his key card was. When he realized he left it on the counter, he knew there was no time to get it. After what seemed like forever, Ford saw the emergency exit sign lit up at the end of the hallway. He sped up, stopping only when he carefully opened the door.

"It hurts…everywhere! What's happening to me, Ford? Am I dying?" Mandy asked.

There was no time to answer. The brisk cold air slapped him in the face while he flew down the steps of the building and raced through the monstrous pile of snow that had cascaded the island within the last couple of days. Ford managed to get any lingering thoughts out of his head before approaching the water.

"What are you doing?" Mandy asked. "Are you trying to kill me?"

"No Mandy, I'm not the one trying to kill you. I'm the one trying to save your life." Ford put her body down onto the snow and rolled her over until the tidal waves crashed against her. He heard her scream one final time before she disappeared into the ocean…

He waited…and waited…and waited. His alter ego ripped his insides, yelling at him to let him free. His eyes searched for her dorsal fin, flukes…anything that told him she had fully transformed into the orca she was supposed to be.

Nothing.

His alter ego roared.

Ford, what the hell did you just do?

CHAPTER TWO

A wave of terror rushed through Mandy while the water invaded her nostrils. She knew dangerous people loved killing their victims through drowning, but this was too much for her. As usual, she had trusted someone who she thought would keep her safe.

She was wrong.

The water filled her lungs with such force, she thought she was dead. But that was nothing compared to the pain she felt inside her body. The horrible cramping made her feel like a statue. The conversation she had with Ford echoed in her brain. She felt her body stretching until it was almost too painful to bear.

What was happening?

It wasn't until the process was complete that her body calmed down. She took a couple of breaths by going to the surface for air before heading back down again. She could see ice drifting into the ocean. She felt herself floating on the water, watching the fish swim by.

The beautiful colors reminded her of a rainbow—full of nothing but extravagant colors invading the ocean.

She couldn't remember anything else after that except for how relaxed she felt while swimming in the water. She reflected on the last time she'd ever felt so warm in this type of environment. When she realized she couldn't remember anything, she put the thought out of her mind and enjoyed the ride.

The next thing she remembered was waking up in that dreadful bed again. Her eyes roamed the room. She was alone. Where was Ford? She shouldn't have cared about the man after what he did to her. She couldn't believe he almost killed her.

She needed to escape.

The other side of her agreed to that decision by giving her a nudge. Mandy checked to make sure she still had feeling in her arms and legs before she sat up on the bed. She became distracted when she heard voices coming from outside the hospital door.

"You were supposed to protect her Ford. If she was transforming, you should have followed her."

"I did go after her Dr. Madison. I didn't know her alter ego was going to take longer than five minutes."

"So how long did you wait before you decided to rescue her huh? Ten, twenty minutes?" Dr. Madison asked.

"I waited until I didn't see her dorsal fin swimming afloat. That's when I decided to take action."

"Do you know how much danger you put her in by waiting? She could have been easily attacked by the other orcas in the ocean, or worse, she could have been attacked by one of the sharks."

Mandy heard silence for a few seconds before Ford responded again. "Even if she sensed any type of danger in the water, her powers would have been able to protect her.

That's what happened to all of us when you injected the Animan Three-Hundred into our bodies. Our powers naturally come out whenever we sense danger, that's part of our nature as Ormans," Ford said.

Mandy swung her legs off the bed and stood up. She felt slightly wobbly from the impact, but she was able to grab the end of the bed frame for support. She inched closer to the door and listened to the conversation.

"You're right, that's part of our nature as Ormans, but according to the rules of Truson, the rules my grandfather wrote—"

"—I know about the rules Dr. Madison. Your grandfather may have published the rules in the *Book of Truson*, but this is still my island. I'm the one in charge of what happens to Mandy and the rest of my team, not you."

"Well, if that's the case, you should act more like a boss than a bystander Ford. Whenever one of your students is in trouble, you're always the first one to respond. Why is it so difficult for you to respond the same way with Mandy?"

"Because I would rather spend time educating my students than spend it focusing on a woman who has no memory of who she is," Ford said.

Mandy took a few steps back from the door. Animan Three-Hundred? Something stirred inside her. How dare they keep secrets that had the potential to cause her death? And what the hell did they inject into her bones? Was that why she was strapped to a hospital bed in the first place?

Mandy went back to her bed and thought about what she needed to do. It had only been forty-eight hours since she woke up not knowing who she was. Now she was in the middle of an argument she couldn't understand. One thing she knew for sure was that she wasn't wanted here.

She needed to leave.

When she heard the doorknob turn, she lay back on her bed and closed her eyes. She then heard the door slam along with stiletto heels clicking against the tile floor.

"With all due respect Mr. Mayfield, I hired you for a reason. I know that her having no memory of who she is is very difficult for you, but I am pretty sure you will be able to handle it." She paused. "Besides her temporary memory loss, she was able to transform into her alter ego with success. It's already been forty-eight hours since I found her dead body washed up on the shores of this island, and she has already proven she's capable of being an Orman and living a successful life as long as she remains on this island."

Ford turned to face Dr. Madison.

"How many times do I need to tell you this?"

Mandy heard Ford scuffing his shoes before he continued.

"You may be a very famous pharmacologist on the other side of town but not here. You're not the boss, I am. I'm the one who teaches the students at the Truson School for Shapeshifters how to survive on their own after the effects of the Animan Three-Hundred. I'm the one who agreed to watch Mandy after you injected her with something you knew might not work after a short time."

Mandy opened her eyes. A flash of ocean blue eyes stared at her. "If you will excuse me, Dr. Madison, my new student just woke up from her long transformation and I would really like to get started. Good night Dr. Madison."

"How dare you dismiss me like this?" she snarled.

Ford broke contact with Mandy and cut his eyes toward Dr. Madison.

"Good night Dr. Madison." Dr. Madison squinted at Ford.

Mandy felt a tremendous level of tension as Dr. Madison stomped her way out into the hallway. The door slammed behind her, causing Ford to give out a nervous smile.

"How much of that did you hear?" he asked.

"Enough for me not to trust you ever again." Ford scratched the back of his head with his finger.

"You do know you have no other choice but to trust me, don't you? You can't leave this island. It's too dangerous for you."

Mandy raised her brow.

"More dangerous than saying you would rather train someone else besides me?"

Ford dropped his head. "That's not what I meant—"

"—If that's not what you meant then why did you say it? You should never say things you don't mean as my parents would say," Mandy said, interrupting him. Ford opened his mouth to speak, but Mandy continued. "You know what? It doesn't matter. I'm not going to stay in a place where I'm not wanted."

Ford exhaled. "You can't leave the island," he repeated. "You don't remember anything. You don't even know your name or how you got here."

Mandy shrugged. Where was this conversation going? "So?"

"I have all of that information for you. Dr. Madison filled me in on who you are. Wouldn't you like to stick around for that?"

Mandy thought about what he said. Something wasn't sitting right with her. Something was missing from this conversation, but she made the mistake of staring at him. Her throat went dry.

"All of that information I can get from Dr. Madison since she's the one who gave it to you," Mandy said.

Ford's expression changed. "Dr. Madison means well, but she's not the boss of Truson Enterprises, I am. What I say goes."

Mandy crossed her arms, causing her bosoms to expose themselves out of the gown. His abdomen stirred. He could feel the blood rushing between his legs. He was getting excited just by looking at her. He needed to stop this. He couldn't afford to be distracted, not when he felt like he was getting somewhere with Mandy when it came to what he wanted.

"Hmmm." Mandy cupped her chin and stared at the ceiling. "That's funny. From the way you guys were talking—I was under the impression Dr. Madison was *your* boss."

Ford inched closer to her. His expression told her she had hit a nerve. What she wasn't expecting was the change in his eyes. The aquamarine suddenly turned into a fiery orange. Mandy looked closer. Flames were shooting out of his irises.

"Dr. Madison is a pharmacologist. She's a person who likes to study dead human and animal cells, mix them together and see what results she comes up with. Although I respect her in her field of choice, she needs to realize her place on the island. I'm the boss of Truson Enterprises which includes running the Truson School for Shape-shifters," he said.

Mandy scoffed. "That's a good statement, but it still doesn't explain why you're keeping me against my will. What is it that you want from me?" Mandy watched his reaction. The expression softened, and Mandy relaxed.

Yeah, she planned to escape from this horrible place after the argument she'd heard, but she needed a plan. The last thing she wanted was for them to stop her from it.

"I want you to do what you are told and stay here on the island until I feel you are ready to leave. Right now, you and I both know you need more rest. We don't want another disaster on our hands like last night."

Mandy tried to remember what happened last night. She remembered the pain she felt inside her body. It was the kind of the pain she'd never experienced in her entire life. Mandy also remembered Ford laying her on the snow.

"Oh, you mean almost killing me?" she said. "What the hell were you trying to do anyway?"

"I was trying to save you. You were transitioning to your orca form or what the team likes to call your alter ego. If you didn't change inside the water, you would have died. I told you that you are no longer a hundred percent human. You're half-human and half-orca which is another word for Ormans."

"It's in your blood now. It's part of who you are," Ford said.

His thumb and his forefinger came together at the bridge of his nose. A part of her wanted him to just apologize for being so irresponsible and scaring her half to death. But the logical part of her thought this whole idea was silly.

There was no such thing as a human turning into an orca or any other animal he was bound to make up. She thought of the many reasons why he would make up a story, but she couldn't find any reason except one.

"Look—" she paused. "What was your name again?"

"Ford."

"Right. Listen, Ford, I don't know why you are making up stories like this. There is no such thing as a human who can transform into an—orca, you call it?"

"Yes," he said. He put his hand inside his pockets. He shifted his weight and locked eyes with Mandy. The physical intensity she felt at that moment traveled through her body.

She shivered.

"Are you cold?"

The question brought her back to the conversation.

"No, I'm fine." She took a moment to figure out what she wanted to say. "Like I was saying, there is no such thing as a human transforming into an orca or any other animal you think of. I just really wish you could be yourself around me." Mandy put her hands on his shoulders. "It's okay. Just say what you mean and tell me who you are. You don't have to impress me."

Ford scoffed. "Impress you? Why would I say all of this to impress you, Mandy? If I didn't know any better, I would say you are calling me a liar."

"Well liars make up stories to suit their needs, don't they?" Ford's jaw tightened at her remark.

"What's wrong? Did I hit a nerve?" Mandy saw the intense look before he turned and headed for the door. *No, you have to stop him. He has the answers you want.* "What's the matter, Ford? Did someone rip your tongue out?"

He paused. Mandy's heart jumped into her throat. Dammit, she couldn't just let him walk out the door, could she? As she wondered why her mouth wouldn't shut up, Ford turned his head.

"No. I tried to be nice and understanding about this situation, but apparently being nice to you is getting nowhere, so you've given me no other choice." He paused. "You are in my care. If you so much as walk off this property, you will regret your decision."

Ford's eyes cut to her. "You need rest, we both do. I will check on you early tomorrow morning."

The door slammed behind him.

Mandy couldn't believe her ears. How dare he tell her what to do? Wasn't she a grown woman who was capable of making her own decisions? Mandy stormed back to her bed. A surge of electricity flooded through her as she tore the pillows in half. Mandy gripped the blanket and was about to throw it across the room when she noticed sprouts of electricity forming around it.

She bent her head forward to get a closer look, and the blanket suddenly exploded into flames. She dropped it and stomped at the orange tentacles, hoping to stop the fire, but more sparks of electricity flicked from her bare feet. Mandy ran back into the wall.

What just happened here?

***

Ford charged down the hallway until he got to the elevators. He couldn't believe what happened. Him, a liar? Never. He always hated liars, especially the ones who lied to other people to get what they wanted. He had experienced the worst kind of liar ten years ago when he found out how his so-called friend decided to go after Roxanne.

It was the worst kind of betrayal he'd ever faced.

Now here he was ten years later being called a liar by a woman who barely knew him. He didn't need to put up with this. Someone else could deal with this garbage, not him. Ford tried to remember the reason why he'd gotten involved in the situation in the first place. He searched for a clock. What time was it? He wondered what the children were doing while he was working on Mandy. Was it lunchtime? He wanted to know what they were doing and how they were adjusting to their new lives.

Just as the elevator doors swung open, Ford heard someone scream. He wasted little time speeding down the hallway, trying to figure out where the voice was coming from.

"Help!" someone screamed between coughs. Ford searched for the voice and saw thick white smoke coming from under the door. With a curse, he ran to the door and placed his hands on the entrance. The flames hadn't reached the door yet.

"Help!" The voice rang out again.

He knew who it was and shifted his weight against the wooden frame. After three tries, he finally managed to push himself inside. Smoke and burnt ashes invaded his face, causing him to cover his nose and mouth. He scanned the room.

She had to be here somewhere.

He was relieved when he saw Mandy crouched in the corner, shielding her face from the smoke by putting her head between her legs. He scooped her up in his arms and bolted out of the room. In the hallway he found his best friend, Stin Vanderson, heading in their direction.

"Are you guys okay?" he asked. His eyes cut from Ford to Mandy. He placed a hand on Ford's shoulder to get his attention. "Are you okay?"

"She's fine." Ford stared at her. "She's just a little shaken up, that's all." Ford tore his eyes away. He knocked down the door. Half of the room had been engulfed in flames. He felt a hand on his shoulder.

"I need to get in there before the room is completely destroyed," Stin said.

Ford nodded. Stin galloped into the room as the students came up the stairs. Ford gained control of the crowd while a massive gush of icy wind enveloped the room, dousing the flames within a matter of minutes.

Damn, Ford already felt guilty about leaving Mandy alone in the room without supervision. Now his students had to come and see the damage left behind.
What the hell was he thinking? Why did he let her get to him to the point where he stormed out of the room, leaving her alone for someone to come and rescue her?

He shook his head. There was no time for self-pity. He needed to know what happened and to find out who was responsible for it.

"Mandy?"

She stared at the wall, not moving, not even to blink her eyes.

"Mandy?"

Finally, she blinked and focused her attention on him.

"Yes?" she asked. Ford saw the fear before her light green eyes flicked into a bright blue halo.

"What happened Mandy? Who did this to you?"

The halo quickly disappeared.

"Mandy, I know you're upset about last night. I get it, but you need to tell me what's going on."

Tears trailed down her freckled cheeks. "No—no one tried to hurt me," she said. "I got upset and ripped the pillows." She sniffed and wiped the tears from her cheeks.

A gush of wind blew on Ford's skin. He shivered. He knew what that meant. Stin was using his powers of snow and ice to fuel the flames. The wind was an indication that the entire room was an icebox, and no one was allowed in unless they wanted to get frostbitten.

"Then I grabbed the cover from the bed. I tried to swing it to the other side of the room. That's when it happened," Mandy said, breaking Ford's thoughts.

"When what happened?"

"I set the place on fire Ford. I nearly destroyed the room!"

Mandy stood up.

"What did you guys do to me after the accident? And what is with these terms I don't understand?" Mandy inched closer to Ford. "Tell me the truth. I need to know everything."

CHAPTER THREE

Ford could have gone on and on about someone trying to murder her. Or he could have gone a different route and told her about who she was, what kind of life she led from childhood until she married the worst man on earth. But he couldn't. Not yet. He knew what he needed to do.

He rubbed her shoulders.

"I know this is hard for you to understand, but I'm not the enemy here. We need to start trusting each other. The only way we can do that is if you do as I say," Ford said. "I won't be able to save you from yourself if you don't."

"What does that mean?" Mandy scratched her head before she massaged her scalp. This whole situation scared her. She didn't know what was going on or what she was doing.

How could she possibly set an entire room on fire? She was losing her mind. She needed to be someplace safe, away from the chains and machines holding her back.

She just wanted to be alone. Her thoughts slowed down as Ford rubbed her back.

"I will explain everything to you I promise. Just not here. There are too many people around. I need to take you somewhere safe."

"Hey, it's Mr. Mayfield!" someone yelled. Ford smiled as his students gathered around him and gave him hugs before some of them noticed Mandy standing next to him.

"Who's she?" One of the students asked. Never removing his hand from her back, Ford tried to inch her forward to no avail.

"This is Mandy, one of the newest members of the Truson Super Elite Team."

Some of the students said hi.

"So, Mr. Mayfield, when are you going to start teaching us again? We miss you, man." The male student put a hand on his shoulder.

"I will be teaching you guys very soon. For right now, I have to make sure my friend Mandy gets well-adjusted to her new life as an Orman." He paused when he saw Stin strolling toward the door.

"Whew. That was some fire," Stin said. "Do you guys know who did it?" Mandy didn't say a word. She couldn't make eye contact with anyone. Weird sensations rocked her entire body as she replayed what happened again in her mind. None of this made any sense. She could feel the tension squeezing at her throat.

She needed air. If she didn't get out of here soon, she was going to have a panic attack.

"Yes. It will be taken care of, don't worry about it," Ford replied and showed his pearly whites to Stin and the students. "As much as I would love to chitchat on this issue, I think Mandy may be feeling a little ill. I'm going to take her someplace where she will feel better." Ford's eyes landed on her. "Are you ready to go?"

"Yes, please get me out of here." Mandy walked down the hall while Stin and Ford stared at each other.

"Mandy, don't go too far please."

Stin looked past Ford's shoulder. "Uh…you might want to go after her dude. She's already ahead of you."

Ford's head turned down the hallway. Dammit, he did it again. He let her escape from his sight. What the hell was the matter with him?

"Ford?" He heard Stin and a few of the other students call his name, but he was far too busy searching for Mandy. His heart raced. Blood rushed through his veins. He thought about the possible scenarios if she were to ever escape the island.

He couldn't afford to let that happen.

Knowing he couldn't wait too long for the elevators, Ford bounded down the stairs, hoping to catch her before she ran out the door. He breathed a sigh of relief when he found her outside the door puking. Ford pushed it open and saw how pale her face looked when she gawked at him. He stuffed his hands in his pockets and leaned out.

"I'm sorry. I wish this transformation was easy for you." Mandy bolted upright.

"Just leave me alone. You can't possibly understand what I'm going through." She grimaced, hunched over and waited until the contents in her stomach landed in the snow.

"Actually, I do know what you're going through. I was much younger than you but not as young as my students when I transformed," Ford said. He walked to where he was within reach before he squatted down.

"Yeah? How old were you?"

"Well, I died when I was in my twenties. Like you, Dr. Madison found me washed up on the Hawaiian shores and decided to fly me back here to the island of Truson." He stood up before extending his arms. "The great island of Truson." Ford put his arms down. "This is the place where Dr. Madison brought me back to life as an Orman."

"Half-human, half-orca," Mandy said. She put her hands on her knees and exhaled.

"You may not know this, but the name 'orca' is the scientific word used to describe what we usually call killer whales."

Mandy nodded. "Right. So how did I become an Orman? I didn't ask for this. Why did Dr. Madison choose me for this stupid experiment? Couldn't she find someone else?"

"That's the first thing that came to mind when I found out who I had become. I didn't like it. Who would want to have a killer whale as an alter ego? That would mean spending some of my time in the water. Why would I want that kind of life?

"Right," Mandy said, lifting a brow.

"But then I quickly realized after Dr. Madison explained it that there were criminals who are also sea animals. They have existed since the Egyptian days. The federal government tried to shield them from making contact with humans for years. They were successful for a while, but within the last twenty years or so, the government decided that keeping them a secret was a bit harder than they realized." The wind suddenly picked up speed. Snowflakes that fell from the darkness tangled with the wind, stinging her face. Ford reached for Mandy.

"I have to take you inside before it gets too cold. May I walk you to my cabin?" Ford asked.

Her light green eyes peered back at him. The sensations she felt the night before bubbled inside again. She felt the tingling sensations flowing through her veins when she laid her hand on his.

***

Ford pushed the feelings out of his mind, but his body was saying otherwise. His alter ego gave him a slight nudge, letting him know he was alert and ready to be out whenever possible. He kept telling himself it was just physical, that after the training and finding the information he needed on who killed his wife, Mandy would be able to leave and go back to the life she wanted, knowing how to control her power when it came to her emotions.

"So, what happened when it became too much to handle?" Mandy said. Ford felt the snow invading his boots, trickling into his socks.

"The federal government decided it was time to take action. They were very successful capturing the Ormans but weren't very smart about keeping them in jail or imprisoning them on the island.

They *needed* to escape so they could transform into their other side to survive." Ford dug into his pockets to look for his keys.

"This is where you're staying?"

Ford glanced at the cabin before he went back to searching for his keys.

"Yes."

"Wow," Mandy said.

"I know," Ford replied.

Where were his keys? He wracked his brain trying to remember when the last time he saw them was. He eventually wrapped his fingers around something in his pocket.

"How long have you lived here?"

He flipped the keys into his hand and used his fingers to separate them until he found the key he was looking for and opened the door.

"Ten Years."

Mandy stepped inside. She caught sight of how beautiful the cottage was and inhaled. Crystal chandeliers full of sparkling real diamonds and jewels hung from the ceiling. The room had a mahogany couch with two small square shaped pillows with unusual patterns of triangles and squares spread throughout the fabric. Mandy stepped closer.

A few inches away from the couch was a small cocktail table made entirely out of glass. Mandy bent down and carefully glided her fingers along the smooth surface.

"You must really like the way it's decorated," Ford said, locking the door behind him.

Mandy shrugged. Her eyes focused on the glass, her own reflection staring back at her. Flashbacks of a little girl in pigtails invaded her thoughts, causing her to lift her hand off the table.

"Are you all right?"

Mandy straightened herself up.

"Yes, I'm fine. You have a beautiful table here." Mandy turned to see a widescreen TV spread from one side of the wall to the other with a huge fireplace underneath. "How long did it take you to decorate?"

"A couple of months." He paused. "Would you like something to eat? You must be starving after the experience you had."

"Uh…no thanks. I think I'm just gonna lie down for a while." Mandy walked a couple of steps toward the stairs but came to a halt when Ford stationed himself in front of her, blocking her from her destination.

"I think you should have something to settle your stomach. It's been two days since you've eaten anything. You need food to build your strength. Come with me please." He turned and led the way into another room. "Are you coming?"

"No," Mandy said. "I'm tired. I just want to lie down." Mandy proceeded to the stairwell. "Which one of the rooms are vacant?" Mandy waited for his response. Her stomach growled.

"If I'm not mistaken, I believe your stomach is telling you otherwise. If you stop being so stubborn and actually listen to what your body is telling you, you won't have any more problems."

"Don't you mean if I listen to what *you're* telling me?" Mandy sassed. "I've only known you for two days, and I'm already starting not to like your attitude."

"Same here," he replied. "Your stomach is growling, I can hear it. You need food to keep up your energy. I'll fix you something healthy to eat. Come."

Mandy wanted to protest, but her stomach didn't. She needed her strength if she was ever going to get out of this place. She had to agree with him on that. Plus, he was holding all the cards to her identity. She needed to know who she was and why Dr. Madison picked her to be an Orman.

So many questions. Not enough answers.

Mandy decided to bury her feelings and try to meet Ford halfway by catching up to him. Their footsteps echoed against the black and white tiled floor as they stepped into the enormous kitchen. The stove, sink, and refrigerator were side-by-side but allowed enough room for lots of active movement. In the middle of the kitchen was a huge marble table that stretched from one wall to the other.

It reminded her of an ER stretcher.

"You can make yourself comfortable by sitting wherever you want," Ford said. "I'm going to start cooking."

"Fine," Mandy said. "Well, can I at least get settled first while you are making dinner? I have a funny feeling I'm going to be staying here against my will for a while."

"Sure. I guess I can give you that option." Ford paused. He thought about how wrong it would be if she were left alone. She'd already hinted at escaping, and there would be too many opportunities for just that. There had to be a way she could stay in the cabin without the chance of her escaping.

Ford grimaced. "Come with me please," was all he could muster. He swiftly moved past her and bolted up the stairs. He glided down the short hallway until he reached the third bedroom at the end. Ford turned the knob and pushed open the door. As soon as they stepped inside, the lights flickered on.

Mandy flopped down on the bed and stared out the window. She could hear Ford enter the room but chose to ignore him, never taking her eyes off of the moonlit waters crashing against the white crested snow. She remembered how good she felt after the transformation process ended and decided she needed to take a shower before settling down to eat dinner with someone who she hardly knew.

Mandy rose to her feet. "If you will excuse me, I'm going to take a shower. It's been a very long day, and I'm going to need plenty of rest after the horrible ordeal I went through." She went past him and found her way to the bathroom, closing the door behind her.

***

He couldn't believe what he saw.

There, perched on a bed was a woman with flowing red hair and eyes that glowed like green crystals on a winter's night.

Although he wanted to hear the conversation between the familiar woman and the unknown man gleaming in the moonlight, Lex Stevenson knew better than to get involved in someone's personal affairs.

Not yet anyway.

"I want you to go to the island and kill someone." His father's words echoed in his ear. The words faded from his mind. He squinted at the couple for a few more minutes before he decided to drag his backpack toward him. He grabbed his binoculars to get a closer look.

He stared at the woman again. *It can't be her. She's dead.* He remembered how upset he was when the police came to the door and told him the news about Mandy. His father shed tears about Mandy's death and how sad it was that her life had to come to such a horrible conclusion.

"It had to be done," Lex remembered the words so clearly. "We needed the money to survive. She had to die."

Now his father was the fool.

Lex shook his head. He didn't want it to be true but had to face reality—Mandy Stevenson was alive and well…

CHAPTER FOUR

Mandy fluffed her hair in the mirror before taking off her clothes. The comments Ford made to her were enough to send her clothes flying across the floor. Electricity surged through her body. She needed to be careful. She didn't want to set the whole place on fire like she did last time.

She took a couple of breaths and smiled as she thought about how she handled herself. She may have lost her memory, but she was smart enough not to let a man get the best of her. She was no pushover, that was for sure. She certainly wasn't going to give Ford or anyone else permission to treat her like crap.

Not anymore. Her mind replayed images of a young woman being slapped and flying across a table. She didn't understand who it was, but it kept coming until she turned on the faucet and stuck her hand under the cold water.

She thought about the images. What could they have possibly meant? Did they hold any value to her identity? And if the woman she saw in her flashbacks was beaten up by someone, why wasn't she able to stop it in time?

The questions kept flooding her mind as she put one foot down in the tub. She quickly got in and put her hair under the shower.

Mandy collapsed against the wall and tried to regain her balance, but her body failed her. The water she'd hoped would soothe her consciousness ended up being her worst enemy. It stung like icicles. Images kept popping faster than before.

A man drowning in a vast pool of water. A little girl who didn't look any older than fifteen or sixteen running toward the beach.

"Don't run in the water. You will get killed." The woman's voice repeated itself.

Mandy kept hearing a buzzing sound as the woman's voice got louder and louder. Her body started vibrating. Flashes of light danced out of her fingertips and onto the tub.

Who was the girl running toward the water? Could it possibly be her? The images of the man drowning in the pool and the woman that told her not to run in the water looked oddly familiar. Could they have been her mother and father? Mandy closed her eyes and said to herself she was okay, that it was all just a horrible nightmare that would eventually go away. She kept her eyes open.

"Okay, relax. These are just stupid dreams, none of them mean anything," Mandy told herself. The familiar rush went through her body. She needed more water. Panicking, Mandy got out of the tub and stared at the mirror.

Black and white patches deepened her features and covered her face. There was a small bump forming on her forehead. Her legs pressed together like glue. She tried her best to pry them open, but they wouldn't budge.

She was transforming…*again.*

She hated to depend on Ford for anything, but Mandy knew she didn't have a choice. She needed him. Mandy wasn't ready to transform yet. She wanted to enjoy a nice long shower and maybe a good meal before falling asleep in a nice cozy bed.

She didn't want this. Ford was right, she bore the image of a half-whale. She was a monster. Knowing the transformation was moving faster by the second, Mandy opened the door before it took hold. She grabbed onto the wall and hopped down the stairs, hearing sounds of laughter.

"Yeah, I know what you mean man. Sometimes these women can be a trip, dude."

"Yes, they can be," Ford said. Who was he talking to? Who was he talking *about?* The transformation was growing stronger. She needed help. She wanted it to stop. She didn't have time for mild trepidations.

She needed him now.

During the transition from the bathroom upstairs to the living room downstairs, she lost her footing and collapsed on the floor with a loud thump. Mandy looked up to see Ford and an unknown man race to her aid.

"Is she transforming?" the man asked as he tried to scoop her off the floor.

"No—wait, she can't be transforming like this. It's too soon," Ford said. The man lifted a brow.

"What do you mean?"

"She transformed twelve hours ago—" Ford cut off his sentence as he lifted her to his chest. The heat radiating through his body sent a wave of emotions through her. She felt her stomach tingle at the close interaction. "—she shouldn't be able to transform again so soon. We need at least twelve hours before we transform or else our human forms will become severely injured."

"So what happens now? What are we supposed to do?" Stin asked.

"We might not have a choice but to send her back to Dr. Madison so she can give her some Binosil to calm her symptoms down."

"What if her symptoms don't go away with the Binosil, dude? We have to think of something else."

"Stin!" Ford barked shortly after he laid Mandy on the couch.

"The Binosil will work, okay? It had worked for us in the past when we transformed. It will work the same way for her as well." Ford took out his cell and punched Dr. Madison's phone number. Luckily, she answered on the third ring.

"Truson Headquarters, this is Dr. Madison speaking, how may I help you?"

"It's me, Ford. I'm going to need your help."

"Why? Is something wrong?" she asked.

"Yes. Apparently, the Animan Three-Hundred is working against Mandy. It's only been twelve hours, and she's transforming again. We need some Binosil so we can reverse the transformation."

"Where is she?"

"She's lying down on the couch and transforming quickly. I would strongly advise you to get over here right now," Ford said.

"I will be there soon. In the meantime, keep Mandy calm. If she does transition before I'm able to take care of her, I'll save her after the transition is complete. Do you know if she's in any pain?"

Ford studied her. The shape of her face and her legs were transitioning. "I don't know for sure."

"What's she's saying, dude? How do we stop the transition?" Stin yelled. "If we don't get her out of here, she's going to die."

He paused. "You need to put her back in the ocean."

"Stin's right," Dr. Madison said. "Just let the transformation happen for right now. I'll probably have to figure out another way to get to her underwater."

"But it's only been twelve hours. If Mandy keeps transforming, her human side won't be able to handle it. There has to be another way," Ford replied.

"Ford, she's getting closer to her full transformation. We've got to get her out of here if we're going to carry her to the ocean."

Ford focused his attention on Mandy. Stin was right.

"Ford, can you please do what Stin and I are asking of you? We know you're the boss, but can you listen and trust my judgment for once?" Dr. Madison pleaded.

"You're right. I need to send Mandy back to the ocean. I'll touch base with you soon." Ford hung up and inched his way toward Mandy. "You grab one side, I'll grab the other. We need to hurry before she gets too heavy."

Stin nodded. He scooted his hands under her backside and lifted one side of her body off the couch. Ford held onto her legs for additional support and carefully walked over to the door.

"Great, how are we going to get her—"

"Switch sides with me." Stin and Ford moved in the opposite direction. Ford stared at the door and searched the room.

"To the ocean?" Stin asked. Ford hated to put Mandy down. If they waited too long, she would turn into an orca and die within minutes.

"I have no other choice. If I don't get Mandy to the ocean soon, she will die. I need to get her to the water as safely as possible." Ford stared at the doorknob and used his powers. *This has to work.* Thoughts of setting the doorknob lose flooded his thoughts.

"What are you doing, dude? We don't have time for this. She's transforming, and here you are trying to test your powers?"

Ford continued concentrating until he saw smoke coming out of the door. *Just a few more seconds…*

"Dude c'mon, we have to—" The doorknob slipped off and landed hard on the floor, interrupting Stin's comments. Still holding Mandy in their arms, they both carried her down the stairs and out into a light snowstorm. Ford was grateful to be an Orman when it came to these types of conditions. The Animan Three-Hundred was able to alter their DNA to survive extreme weather temperatures like the ones they experienced now.

"She's getting heavier, dude. We have to put her in the water.

It's not looking too good."

"Put her down," Ford said. "Stomach first. It'll be easier for her to float when her body touches the water." Ford and Stin carefully laid Mandy down. Her body formed into her alter ego the moment the water hit her. Soon she floated onto the ocean and disappeared underneath. Ford wasted little time getting undressed while challenging his alter ego to come out full force.

"Hey man, I love you but not like that!"

"Stin, I have to follow her to see if she's safe. You're more than welcome to join me if you like or you can stand there like an idiot. It's your choice." The blood mixed in with his supernatural strength took force.

"Naw man. I think I should go back to my students. They're probably waiting for me right now." Ford and Stin gazed at the massive building that looked about as tall as the Willis Tower on a snowy slope. Ford wanted to protest but decided now wouldn't be a good time to argue and dove into the water.

***

Lex and some of the other students from the Truson School for Shapeshifters hurried back into the classroom with Dr. Madison's encouragement. Once all of the students got settled in their seats, Dr. Madison stood in the middle of the room and cleared her throat.

"I'm sorry about the confusion around here. I know it may seem like things are a little chaotic right now—"

"Chaotic isn't the word for it. I want to know what's going on. Why isn't Mr. Vanderson here? Where is he?" Lex asked. Some of the other students piped in, supporting Lex.

"I know this is very confusing for all of you, but I'm sure if you can all be patient for just a little bit longer, Mr. Vanderson will be back from his short visit and classes will resume as normal."

One of the students scoffed. "And what exactly do you call 'normal'? Nothing in this situation is normal. Mr. Mayfield is not here because he's dealing with some girl we don't know, Mr. Vanderson is off doing God knows what and now we have you standing here, telling us to calm down. We're not stupid, Dr. Madison. We want to know what's going on."

The other students rallied in protest. Lex nodded and watched Dr. Madison hold her hands up.

"You're right Abdullah, you guys all need to know what's going on, but I'm pretty sure Mr. Vanderson will fill you in on the details. For right now, I just want you to be as patient as possible and continue whatever it was you were doing."

"And what if we don't do as you say?" Lex asked, challenging her decision.

Dr. Madison twitched. "Do you really want to challenge my authority on that one?" She took a couple of steps toward him.

Lex never moved. He wasn't scared of her. Even though Lex was born an albino, it didn't mean he was a punk. Considering who his father was, being scared of anything wasn't an option. If there were even a hint of fear in his eyes, his father would beat it out of him until he was satisfied.

"Lex, you really don't want to mess with a woman like me. I'll make you regret it." They were basically nose-to-nose. Lex's blood boiled. He sensed his alter ego coming out. His powers were forming.

Come on, test me. I dare you.

"Yo Lex, it's not worth it. You just got here. Don't screw it up," one of the other students said.

"I would strongly advise you to listen to what your peers are telling you."

Lex stared at her for a few moments while trying to calm himself. It wasn't until one of his friends grabbed his shoulder that he broke eye contact and sat in the chair behind him. He searched the room to see if the other students followed suit.

They eventually did.

Just as Dr. Madison was about to speak, Stin came through the door.

"Hey, you guys, sorry I'm so late. I had to deal with an emergency," Stin said. He turned to Dr. Madison.

"Thanks for filling in for me. I believe I can take it from here."

"Good, cause I thought I was going to lose it for a second." Dr. Madison waved good-bye and left the room.

"Sorry about that my future Ormans. I had to take care of something." Stin looked at his watch. He swung his head back and forth, trying to figure out if he should let the class go early.

"So, what are we doing now?" Lex asked.

Stin clapped his hands together. "You know what? I think we should do an hour of training and then we'll be done for the day, okay? How does that sound?"

Lex shrugged. "Cool." He couldn't have cared one way or another. His mind was too focused on what he saw earlier. Images of the woman with the bright curly red hair invaded his thoughts. He wanted to feel sorry for her. His mind continued to fool him about seeing things, that the woman who stood in that window the other night wasn't the same woman who he used to call his stepmother. Somehow, his instincts told him otherwise.

He couldn't shake that feeling.

"Come with me, everyone. We're going to the gym." Lex let the other students line up before he finally had the strength to move to the back of the line. Some of the students were talking about how the rest of the day was going to be spent after training was over. "Okay, let's go guys." As Lex and his classmates walked toward the gym, a bunch of teenagers started discussing the pep rally and the exams that were coming up within the next few weeks.

Mr. Vanderson turned and stared at the back of the line. "Keep the noise level down. Other students are trying to study in the classroom." After seeing the mysterious woman talking to Ford earlier, in addition to following his father's orders about killing Ford, Lex was on a mission and from the way things were heading, he knew he was on the right track. As some of the students headed toward the gym, Lex felt his phone vibrate in his pocket. He gripped it until everyone turned the corner then he went toward the window and picked it up.

"Hey, Dad, what's up?"

"Don't hey Dad me, you fool!" he barked into the phone. "Have you found Ford Mayfield yet?" Lex swallowed. He knew by the tone of his father's voice he wasn't in a good mood.

When has he ever been in a good mood?

"No Dad, I haven't. I've only been here for two days. I haven't had time to do much of anything considering the level of security."

"Well you need to do something about this and soon because if I get one more visit from Samuel and his pesky sidekicks from the Transforments, your ass is on the line."

"Dad, I'm working as hard as I can to figure out where he is. I get Samuel's on your back, but I need to make sure they don't see me as a target," Lex said. "I'm sorry Dad, I have to follow the rules."

"Don't you talk back to me like that you albino freak. I need you to do as I say and find Ford Mayfield so we can send his body back to where he belongs—in a grave next to me," he said.

Lex heard his father chuckling at his own statement. "And you will Dad. You just have to give me some more time."

"Time for what?" A familiar voice asked. Spooked by the sound, Lex saw Mr. Vanderson leaning on the rail peering at him.

"Where are your other students? Shouldn't you be more focused on them?" Still holding the phone in his hand, Lex could hear his father on the other line asking who he was talking to.

Mr. Vanderson reached for the phone.

"I think I should remind you about the use of cell phones. We're not allowed to have them in the buildings during regular school hours."
Lex clenched his jaw. He didn't want to give up the phone, it was the only way to communicate with his father.

"But I need my cellphone in case of an emergency," Lex said, hoping it would sway the teacher.

Mr. Vanderson shook his head.

"If there is an emergency, I'm pretty sure someone will be able to call the office." Mr. Vanderson still had his hand out, waiting on Lex to hand the phone over. "The phone please."

Lex scoffed. He knew there was a possibility he could get into a lot of trouble for handing it over, but what other choice did he have? If he didn't, he was going to get suspended which would delay his father's plans.

Lex tossed the phone to Mr. Vanderson and leaned against the wall.

"I'm curious to know who you were talking to. I know it's none of my business, but I heard a name I'm familiar with. Can we talk about it?"

Lex pushed himself off the wall and grabbed the rail on the other side of the stairs.

"You're right Mr. Vanderson, it's none of your business." Lex flew down the stairs and strolled to the gym.

Mr. Vanderson wasn't too far behind him. Lex could hear his low heel clicking against the tiled floor.

Lex turned. "Do you have to follow me around everywhere I go?"

Mr. Vanderson shrugged.

"It's part of my job. I'm your teacher for the time being. I have to make sure everyone is safe and happy."

"If you have to make sure everyone is safe and happy, who is in the gym while you're standing here talking to me?"

"One of the security guards who usually monitors the hallways is watching them until I get back. Are you sure you don't want to talk about the phone conversation you just had?"

"Go to hell," Lex said. Who did he think he was asking him a question like that? He didn't have to explain himself.

"Wow, is that the way you talk to your teachers? If it is, we're going to have to do something about it." Lex was glad to make it to the gym with his peers so Mr. Vanderson could shut up. He'd only been here for forty-eight hours, and already he wanted to leave this place behind and go home.

But he needed to stay. He needed to figure out once and for all if the red-head woman was who he first thought. If she was the woman he suspected, that would definitely pose a problem for both of them…

CHAPTER FIVE

As Ford woke up the next day in his own bed, he couldn't remember what exactly happened between him and Mandy, but he knew whatever they experienced undoubtedly felt right to him. He stretched his arms out to the side and rolled over. Ford rubbed the bed sheet and opened his eyes once he realized no one else was in bed with him. He tried to remember what happened the night before when his stomach growled.

With the little memory he had as an orca, he knew he had eaten a lot of fish to squelch his appetite, but it wasn't enough. No matter. He had enough food to last for the next several days. He sat up in bed.

Where is she? His mind wondered what else had happened since he'd dived in and transformed into his alter ego. After the stunts she'd pulled in the last two days, he couldn't trust leaving her alone. There was too much at stake. He shifted his weight off the bed and stood up. He stretched his arms again and looked at the bed once more. He sighed. For the first time since his wife died, he wished he hadn't spent the night alone. He grimaced.

You would have liked for her to sleep with you, huh? That thought made him hard. Another blood rush. His alter ego wanted to come out but not in the way he expected.

This wasn't good.

His stomach growled again, interrupting his thoughts. He got up and found a t-shirt and some jeans before he gawked at the rugged appearance in the mirror. He shrugged and stepped out of his bedroom and decided he would search the living room first for Mandy.

"Good morning," a voice boomed from behind. Ford turned and saw vibrant, sparkling green eyes staring back at him. His feelings stirred inside him. He felt himself getting to the peak of explosion. *Get a grip, Ford.*

He straightened.

"Good morning." He gave her a smile indicating whatever happened the night before was long gone. "Did you get a good night's rest? I hope that whatever happened last night didn't disturb you."

Mandy scratched the back of her head.

"Well, that's the thing. I don't exactly remember what happened last night."

"It's okay. I don't remember much of anything either. I don't think we're supposed to. Dr. Madison said something about our brains functioning differently whenever we transition from human to orca." Ford shook his head.

"What's with you when it comes to this Dr. Madison woman?" Mandy asked.

Ford raised a brow.

"What do you mean?" He made his way past her and headed for the stairs. He was starving and the way Mandy looked after she woke up from her sleep was doing things to him, he wasn't fond of.

Mandy followed after him.

"I've noticed some tension between you two ever since I got here. It seems like fighting is a daily occurrence." Mandy paused. Ford took out the items stored in the fridge and placed them on the counter. "It almost seems like you guys have a brother/sister type relationship."

Ford thought about the idea. "You could say that. I know Dr. Madison means well, she always has. After all, it was she who took care of us after her father injected the Animan Three-Hundred into our bodies." Ford bent down and grabbed a frying pan from the cabinet and started the fire before he continued. "She even stepped up her role as our teacher once Benjamin Truson died."

"How?" Mandy asked.

"A couple of days after Benjamin transformed, he died from a fatal disease. Dr. Madison stepped up, and for a while she was the only teacher we had so we learned a lot from her." Ford poured a small amount of olive oil into the pan.

"Like what?" Mandy asked. She walked over to the table and sat down. "Did she teach you all of the weird stuff that's going on with me now?"

Once the pan was covered, Ford gently placed it on the stove and got four eggs out of a carton. He put the eggs into a glass bowl and shoved the container back into the refrigerator.

"I don't understand what you mean."

"Like the electricity and stuff. I mean, I've been angry before, but usually, I was able to trash a room and not suffer any consequences. Now it just seems like…" Mandy cut herself off. "I don't know why I believe all of this. This kind of stuff doesn't exist in the real world. People don't just transform into animals. It's not possible."

"I used to think the same way you do," Ford said. "How do you like your eggs?"

"Eggs over easy please."

Ford nodded and cracked the eggs into the skillet.

"Anyway, I used to tell Dr. Madison about it all the time. At first, I thought it was just some scheme they created so I couldn't go back to the life I wanted." Ford shuffled his weight and searched inside the freezer until he found the frozen T-bone steak he stored the night before to defrost. He took it out.

"So, what changed your mind? What made you finally start believing all of this was real?" Ford stopped and hunched over the sink. Memories of what happened to Roxanne flashed through his mind. He wasn't ready to talk about what happened…not yet.

If not now, then when, Ford? On your deathbed? Ford ignored the thought.

"When someone significant to me died," was all he could muster before he focused his attention back on the steak. He prayed she wouldn't ask any more questions when it came to his personal life.

"Oh," Mandy replied. "I would love to know who, but I really don't want to start that discussion."

"Yes, I appreciate that." Ford put the seasoning on the steak before putting it into an aluminum pan and shoving it into the oven. He whirled around as reminisces of last night swirled his brain.

"By the way, I don't think I apologized for my behavior. I shouldn't have gone off on you like I had. It was insulting and disrespectful. The people that truly know me would say what I did was completely out of character, so I do apologize." Ford's eyes roamed over her body.

Now it was her turn to shift in her seat.

"Apology accepted," she finally said. Ford smiled. He had a feeling she was getting a little comfortable around him. He grunted.

"What's wrong? And why are you staring at me like that?" Mandy asked.

He hadn't even realized he was staring at her until now.

"Where was I? I think you wanted to know how the relationship between me and Dr. Madison started, correct?"

"And why you are so mean to her after everything she's done for you?" Mandy asked.

Ford nodded. "I don't consider myself a 'mean' individual. I will admit I can be very contemptible and strict when it comes to getting what I want. Don't get me wrong, Dr. Madison is excellent as a pharmacologist but not as a leader."

Mandy's eyes widened.

"We have a lot of ancestors who have been here before the humans were even thought about." Ford tried to keep a straight face but smiled when she started to become fascinated by what he was saying.

"That's impossible. I don't believe you."

"It's true."

Mandy rolled her eyes. "Whatever," she said. "How long have you guys been on earth?"

"Since the Egyptian times. I don't know exactly when they first found out about us." Ford got up from his chair and checked the eggs before he turned off the stove and poured them onto the plate. "All we know is that there was an Egyptian name Hasina who stole this special potion from one of the kings in Egypt."

"Oh, my. Did Hasina ever get caught?"

Ford turned and shrugged.

"I don't remember. You're going to have to read the *Book of Truson* to find out."

He took out the seasoning.

"Do you want anything on your eggs?"

"Salt and pepper," she replied.

Ford did a light sparkle on the eggs and placed the plate on the table.

"Thank you."

"No problem," Ford said. He sat back in his spot. When he saw Mandy searching for silverware, he grabbed it from inside one of the drawers and handed it to her. She dug into the egg and moaned.

Ford's heart raced. *Wow, what would it be like if she looked at me that way?*

"Good?" he asked, distracting himself from his thoughts.

She nodded, her mouth apparently too full to make any suggestions. He remembered the last conversation they left off. "Dr. Madison never told you about the *Book of Truson*, has she?"

Mandy swallowed what was left of her egg. "She didn't tell me much of anything before she decided to whisk me away to this place. All I knew was she injected me with a potion, that's it. I didn't even see what she looked like until you two had that argument."

"There are so many things I must teach you. I don't know where to begin." Ford paused while Mandy took another bite. "I was unprepared for this. I had planned to teach my high school students how to control their powers and to research their own kind. I never suspected I was going to teach someone far older."

"Meaning what?" Mandy asked. "How old do you think I am?"

Ford folded his hands. "I know how old you are actually. Dr. Madison gave me quite a bit of information on you before you awakened."

"Really? What kind of information did she give you?" Ford was about to answer when he heard a knock at the door. He huffed when he saw Dr. Madison on the other side, smiling.

"Good morning, Ford. How are you feeling today?" she asked. Dr. Madison walked into the living room.

Ford closed the door. "I'm excellent, Dr. Madison. I would probably be better if I didn't get constant visits from you. Checking up on me again?"

Dr. Madison peered into the kitchen and stepped inside. "Hello Mandy, how are you feeling today?" she asked, completely ignoring Ford's question. Ford grunted. He always hated being ignored.

"Better, considering the delicious food Ford has cooked for me this morning." Mandy made eye contact with him and smiled. His body reacted again. *You need to stop doing this to yourself. She already has a life, remember?*

"That's great. I'm glad Ford was able to provide that for you," Dr. Madison said. She clapped her hands together. "Did he help you yesterday as well?"

Ford closed his eyes in disgrace. Apparently, someone had to be watching them last night. He reviewed in his head how many bodyguards were around the building. Too many to count. He hung his head.

Mandy shrugged.

"He's been helping me out since I woke up from the hospital bed."

Dr. Madison glared at Ford.

"Did you transform at all last night?" Dr. Madison asked, pressing the issue.

"Just get to the point, please. Did someone suggest something to you?"

"I suppose you didn't do your job and go with her into the ocean last night, did you?" she asked.

"It's nice you think so little of me." Ford grabbed a pair of gloves off the rack and checked on the steak.

"I don't want to think this way, Ford. I know you're a terrific guy to handle these types of situations, but I really need you—"

Ford slammed his fist on the table.

"For your information, I was right by her side when she transformed. Stin wanted to stay, but he needed to go back inside and finish teaching the class." He paused. "I don't owe you an explanation for what I do. I'm *your* boss, you're not mine."

Mandy raised her hand.

"Permission to intervene?"

Ford and Dr. Madison fell silent.

"Dr. Madison, you're a little harsh on Ford, don't you think?" Mandy glared at Ford. "I thought I was in a lot of danger with him at first but now—" Mandy shrugged. "We're okay now. I still may have my doubts about him when it comes to his behavior, and I can't say I trust him completely yet, but we're getting there."

Dr. Madison gave a smile.

"It seems like your relationship is improving. I just wish Ford had informed me about what went on sooner."

"Why?" Mandy asked. "Why are you so invested in my recovery all of a sudden? It seemed like you weren't invested before."

"That's not true. I was always invested in your recovery—that's the whole reason why I paired you two up—" Dr. Madison paused. "Not in a literal sense because we all know what happens if two Ormans get together regarding being partners in a business sense."

"We know what you meant Dr. Madison. Can you please explain your reasons for being here because so far, I don't hear anything worth you interrupting us. I have many things planned for Mandy and me. The last thing I need to hear right now is another lecture from someone who is supposed to be studying cells and doing her job."

Dr. Madison squinted but focused on Mandy again.

"I want you to be informed about what's going on. Anyway, I must say I'm fairly surprised by what happened last night. I think her transforming twice within a short period of time is a real problem."

"I don't see what the problem is. Ford took good care of me. I have to admit I wasn't in any danger because Ford was by my side." Dr. Madison relaxed.

"Good…good." She nodded and gave a small grin. "I'm glad he didn't leave you out in the ocean like before."

"Why? Is there something I need to know?" Ford asked. Dr. Madison exhaled. Her eyes averted from Ford to Mandy and back again.

What the hell was going on? Ford knew by her expression she'd received some sort of news that involved Mandy she didn't want to share.

Could it be that he was finally getting closer to the truth? Could it be possible that they were one step closer to finding who was responsible for Roxanne's death? If so, things were about to change dramatically. He wasn't exactly sure if he was ready for what Dr. Madison would reveal to him.

He wasn't sure if he was ready for anything anymore.

Ford could tell Dr. Madison wanted to respond but was too afraid to say anything in front of Mandy. He understood. The last thing he wanted was for her to know Dr. Madison only sent him to find out the truth about what happened to his wife.

Ford thought about how he was going to get the information without Mandy knowing the truth. He had to figure out a way to distract her so Dr. Madison could reveal her secret…

***

Mandy gawked at Dr. Madison and Ford staring at each other. She shivered, not liking the way they were looking at each other. Ford's eyes grew with intensity. Her alter ego grunted.

You stay away from him, he's mine.

The thought staggered her. Where the hell did that come from? She had only met this man three days ago, and she was marking her territory already. Had she officially lost her mind? None of this made any sense. First, she had an awful dream about a man she didn't know—something she wanted to reveal to Ford but didn't have the opportunity before Dr. Madison jumped in.

Her feelings were all mixed up.

One thing she couldn't shake off was the silence that filled the room. Mandy couldn't help but be nosy about what they were hiding because of the glances she got from Ford and Dr. Madison.

"What's going on? Why are you guys staring at me like that?"

Ford cleared his throat, breaking the silence. "We'll talk about this later. Right now, I really want to get started on Mandy's training. We've already delayed it for the last three days. I don't want to delay it any further."

Ford smiled.

Electricity rushed through her veins. *When will these feelings ever cease?*

Mandy snapped out of her thoughts.

"We haven't finished breakfast yet," Mandy said. *In other words, I want to know what you're hiding.*

And to spend more time looking at him in his rugged white shirt and black pants.

"Of course." Dr. Madison nodded. "Of course." She paused. "I think I should go. I didn't mean to interrupt your breakfast. I was just checking on you, especially on a day like today." Ford's expression changed. More questions swirled in her mind as Dr. Madison excused herself and was escorted out of the cabin. It wasn't until the door closed that he moved back to the kitchen.

"What is she talking about?" Mandy pressed. "You know, we talked a lot about the Truson S.E.T., which is nice, but isn't it time we got to know each other a little bit better?"

"I'm surprised you haven't asked me about who you are." Ford managed to sit down at the table. He picked up his fork and knife and started cutting the steak. "As a matter of fact, I'm surprised Dr. Madison didn't mention anything about your amnesia." He took a bite off the steak and smiled. "Perfection."

Mandy was silent for a while. Amnesia? She wouldn't have guessed why she couldn't remember anything.

"I have amnesia?" Mandy asked. "How long do you think it will last?"

"It depends on your condition. Although I'm hoping it's only temporary, I'm not quite sure how long it will be before your memory returns." He positioned the steak on a plate and presented it to Mandy.

"Do you think my memory will ever return?"

"Maybe," Ford said. He gave himself a hefty serving of steak before he settled into the chair facing Mandy. "But for right now, I just want you to keep your strength. You need to eat a lot of food today because you're going to need it for what I have planned for you."

Mandy leaned forward. "And what exactly do you have in store for me?" she asked.

"Today is your first day of training."

CHAPTER SIX

The first day of training?

Mandy pondered the response in her head. *Training?* She thought about the two incidents she already suffered due to her emotional outbursts. Could they be connected somehow?

"Training," she said and sank farther into her chair. "What kind of training?"

"The type of training where you learn to control your emotions." Ford took a couple of bites from his plate.

"Who am I?" Mandy asked. "The only information you have given me so far is my name, that I was in a horrible car accident and that I'm an Orman."

"I told you what you needed to know at the time." Ford took another bite. "I'm surprised it took this long for you to ask that question."

Mandy scoffed. "Excuse me if I wanted to know why I was turning into a killer whale every few minutes."

"The proper term is orca. We don't say killer whales even though they are known to kill other sea animals for food. We still think it's disrespectful to call them that. However, since the name 'Orman' came from the word human and orca…" Ford paused. "We Ormans take the name seriously."

"I see." Mandy's eyes widened at his statement. She thought that Ford was a little sensitive about the whole matter, but she really wasn't up for an argument with him. She continued eating and repeated the question.

"From what we know so far, your name is Mandy Jane Stevenson. You were born in Vemmit City, New Jersey. Your parents are very wealthy. They bought a huge mansion steps away from the Vemmit River. Your father owned a couple of boats out there."

"Really?" She closed her eyes to see if she could remember anything.

"See anything yet?"

"No."

"Don't worry. I'm sure you'll probably remember it all real soon," he said and paused.

Mandy stared at the softness in his eyes as a smile formed on his lips. Her throat went dry. Why did he look at her like that? She felt the tingles growing in the pit of her stomach. At this rate, she wasn't going to remember much of anything.

Heaven help her.

"Hope so," was all she could muster before taking another bite. "So, what else do you know about me?"

He shrugged. "You lived a pretty decent life. You were going to school to become a psychologist. Your mom and dad talked you into going out on dates and finding the right man to marry." Ford shook his head at the thought. "I don't know if I'm explaining it right. It sounds weird. Why would any parent try to marry their children off before they were ready?"

"Inheritance I believe." She grimaced.

"Really? How would you know that?" He leaned forward, his eyes focused on her. Her heart felt like a ticking time bomb every time they were close to each other, every beat going harder and faster until she felt like she was going to explode. She broke eye contact and stared at the steak. Why did his shiny light blond hair and ocean blue eyes make her feel this way?

"Mandy, did you hear me?"

The intensity she felt around him made her weak.

"I think we should get started on our training now."

"I'm sure there's a lot you want to teach me when it comes to this Orman superpower stuff," Mandy said and watched Ford shift his weight.

"I guess you're right." He sat back. "We have a lot we need to focus on." He extended his hand. "Plate?"

Mandy gave the plate to Ford, causing him to get up and start washing the dishes. Mandy was relieved when she pushed her chair back and got up from the table. Him being so close to her wasn't doing her any favors. She needed to focus on something that didn't involve having sex with a total stranger.

Easier said than done.

"So, what are you going to teach me today?"

Ford quickly washed the plates and stored them in the dish rack before shutting off the water and wiping his hands on the towel.

"What's the plan?" Mandy asked.

"Well, I wanted to start you with the basics first. I was going to do a swim test to see if you can actually swim, but I think we'll wait on that considering what happened within the last few hours."

You think? Mandy smiled. She'd hoped Ford didn't pay any attention to her as he continued the conversation.

"We'll start with controlling your emotions. I know the other two nights seemed a little scary to you when I rolled you into the water."

"A little scary? I thought I was dying."

"You were fine," Ford said. You made it through the transition quite well." Silence passed between them before he picked up the conversation again. "Is there anything you would like to do before we leave for the Truson School?"

Mandy wondered what she needed. She was afraid to take a shower alone after the last incident. If she wanted another one, it would require Ford watching her every move.

Would love that, wouldn't you?

"If you're thinking about taking a bath, I would strongly advise you against it. You're going to work up a sweat during training."

"Don't worry, I haven't thought about it after the last incident. Shall we get started?"

"Excellent idea," he said. He stood off to the side.

Mandy walked into the living room and waited for Ford. Soon they were outside on the island, their footwear halfway covered in snow. Relief flooded through her when she glanced at her feet.

She was too tired from the night before to do much of anything. They trudged through the deep snow, each step worse than the last. Light white-crested snowflakes gently massaged Mandy's face while she followed Ford. She sighted a silvery white glow cascading over the ocean and smiled. Images of a little girl splashing her feet in the water invaded her mind. Was that *her* playing in the water? She saw the same physical features—red hair, light green eyes, small freckles around her cheeks—as the picture continued playing in her mind. It was such a beautiful image, the little girl giggling and smiling while she stared out into the river.

"Mandy?"

As the image began, her mind switched to another picture—this time to a man who seemed unfamiliar. She heard Ford call her name again but decided to ignore it. The model revealed a man buried deep in the water, gasping for air. Mandy's heart pounded. She could hear the screams etched in her mind. Once the man tried to come up for air, he was blue…

"Mandy!"

The image faded away like dust.

"What?"

"We're here."

Mandy shifted her focus to the enormous building perched on a hill. It looked like a typical school building—old gray windows and doors stared back at her. The sign titled "Main Entrance" hung on the door like the plaque. Mandy scowled. She felt like she was back in high school all over again.

"This is where we're going to be training?"

Ford nodded. "I know it may look like those typical elementary schools you're used to seeing on a daily basis, but I guarantee you, there's more to the Truson School for Shape-shifters. Come," he said. He continued walking with Mandy following close behind him. Ford took out his card and swiped himself into the building. He held the door for her before it closed shut behind her.

Mandy searched the main entranceway and couldn't believe what she saw. The ceiling was stunning. Dome-shaped, it was surrounded by small LED lights and holograms of dolphins, orcas, and other sea animals. It literally took her breath away. She felt like the animals were staring back at her, greeting her with a warm smile.

"I see the ceiling has captured your attention. It took the whole team two years for it to look the way it does now."

"Wow," Mandy said.

"I know. I'm very proud of my students and my team. They worked really hard on it." He paused. "Come, we have much to do. We are getting closer to being late for our first lesson."

Ford backed away. He positioned himself behind Mandy and placed his hand on her back, motioning her to move forward. Mandy knew the gesture was insulting, but it didn't stop her from wanting more. Mandy's alter ego jumped for joy. She tried to think of something to prevent her sexual urges from going too far.

"This is the grand foyer of the entire school. I guess we could take a brief tour before we start," Ford said.

"No, I need to start the training now. I can see the rest of it later." She needed to get away from him. She needed space. The only way it was going to happen was if she finished the training A.S.A.P.

"Okay, I guess we can do the training now. Are you sure everything's okay? You did space out for a minute."

"I'm fine," Mandy said. She didn't want to say or do anything else until they started the training. They remained silent as they walked toward the end of a vast hallway on the other side of the building. Ford punched in a few numbers, and the door flew open.

This room wasn't so glamorous.

Metal doors were covering the entire walls. The only thing that didn't look so bleak was the hardwood floors zigzagging throughout the room. The place felt like more of a dungeon than a central foyer.

"It feels like a prison in here." Mandy rubbed her arms. "It's cold. I'm surprised the heat wasn't on when we first entered."

"It will be on very soon. Don't worry about the decorations in here. The metal is here for a reason, trust me."

Before Mandy spoke another word, Ford took his hands and formed them into a ball, his fingers barely touching each other. Suddenly, a flicker of flames shot out from his fingers and swirled around in the middle of his palms until it formed into a ball. Ford released one hand and put it behind his back. The ball spun like the Earth in his hand.

Mandy watched Ford's eyes grow more intense. The little fireball spun faster. Mandy swallowed hard. She didn't like the way it was going. She took a couple of steps back. Soon Ford put the other hand behind him, causing the ball to spin in mid-air. Mandy focused on it until Ford flicked it with the back of his hand. The ball made a massive echo across the entire gym.

Mandy held her breath, waiting for the place to engulf in flames.

Nothing happened.

The ball exploded into a small pile of dust and landed on the floor. She thought her mind might have been playing tricks on her, but the ashes held the evidence of what happened.

"If you're still wondering if the place is going to explode, don't hold your breath," Ford said. "This place is anti-inflammatory. The only way it could go down is if a gush of water run through it."

Mandy lifted her brow.

"I guess Stin is banned from here huh?" Before Ford could respond, Mandy continued. "Even if someone set a bomb to this whole entire building, it wouldn't move?"

"No, that's not the whole building. It's just for this room. This room was designed for this type of training. It's made of nine hundred tons of steel and metal. If there were an emergency, this would be the place to feel safe and warm."

"Except for maybe a hurricane or a Tsunami, right?" she asked.

Ford scoffed.

"We're still trying to work on that one." He grimaced at the unsettling thought, causing Mandy to smile. She was starting to get to know him well. She made a mental note about him talking too much while she waited for what the next step was.

"What I just demonstrated to you is my supernatural ability which is fire. Your supernatural ability is electricity. Although I don't understand the difference now, we shall soon see the similarities and differences between us." They were only inches apart. The feeling of rummaging her fingers through his hair invaded Mandy's body.

Need to stop thinking like this. What's the matter with you? Focus.

"Shall we?" Ford crossed his arms in front of him. She nodded.

"Great! Let's begin." Ford clapped his hands together. Mandy thought of what Ford had said about her going to school to become a psychologist. Though she didn't remember much about her job, it was starting to make sense to her based on the one thought that kept invading her mind.

What exactly was Ford Mayfield hiding?

***

"Everyone, close your eyes and try to think about something that makes you happy."

Stin walked down the small row of teenagers to see if they were responding to him. He was surprised they were after being assigned their substitute teacher a couple of days ago. He wasn't pleased about taking the job at first, even after Dr. Madison pleaded with him several times to take it. He just wanted to spend his days surfing along the Arctic shores of Truson to prepare for a major contest they were having on the island.

Twenty-three surfers (himself included) signed up to surf the highest waves imaginable to win one of the top prizes—a two-thousand-dollar gift card to spend on whatever they wished.

But he wasn't in it for the money…not at all.

Stin and the rest of the members were very wealthy indeed. As being a part of the Truson team, they always got a *very* huge salary to satisfy their living conditions. Stin's bank account was so huge it would make anyone jealous he was even born. It was enough for him to live out the rest of his days as a surfer.

That was all he wanted…to live the dream of a surfer.

Unfortunately, the contest seemed to be fading from his view. He grunted. Why the hell did Dr. Madison have to choose this particular moment to try this experiment on someone else? Couldn't she have waited until he got the award before she went searching for another member of the team?

"Now stretch your arms out in front of you, palms facing up, eyes closed." He paused. Thoughts about Dr. Madison and her latest experiment infuriated him. He tried to calm himself down by thinking about his best friend Ford and why he was teaching these snot-nosed teenagers in the first place. "I want you to form an image that represents happiness."

"Like what?" one girl asked.

Stin paced up and down the row. "You're going to imagine an object that represents your sense of happiness. It could be any object you want. A ball, a jump rope, a cloud…the list is endless." Stin carefully watched them concentrating and listening to every word he said. He had to admit how amazing it was to see them sucking up his words of wisdom considering how he didn't prepare a lesson plan for the whole week.

This teaching thing seemed comfortable enough. Why did he have to do extra paperwork to plan an activity for them to do? Stin's thoughts about lesson plans came to a halt when his eyes turned to a teenage boy who he recognized hanging out in the hallways during the transition period. His arms were folded, his black hood covered most of his face. From the way he was positioned, Stin thought the boy was sleeping while standing.

What was this kid's name again?

Stin continued his pace around the room until he stopped where the boy was. He opened his mouth, trying his best to tell the boy to take off his hoodie when he heard someone screaming his name.

"Stin! Stin, do you have a second? I need your help with something."

Stin huffed. He really wasn't in the mood to talk to someone he found utterly annoying. Regrettably, he turned and stared into those hideous light brown eyes and pretended he wasn't irritated at being interrupted.

"Yes, Tonia? I'm in the middle of something right now. Can you please make this quick so I can get on with my lesson?"

"And hello to you too."

Stin watched her put her hands on her hips and yawn. "I don't mean to be a bother to you or to your fellow students, but I need to know where Ford is."

"Probably someplace where he's not being stalked by you." Stin heard some of the students giggling at his harsh statement.

"For your information *Stin,* I'm not stalking him. I need to know where he is so I can give him some information," Tonia replied.

Stin put his hands in his pockets and rocked on his heels. "Really? This ought to be interesting. What information could you possibly have that's so urgent Tonia? Did your hair catch on fire? Did the wind shield you from losing your powers? I could go on, but I don't want to bore myself with the meaningless possibilities of your visit."

Stin saw the flash of green in her eyes, a sign her alter ego wanted to come out and rip him to shreds.

"Way to tell her off Mr. V," one of the male students said. A female student shoved her elbow into his chest, a clear sign she was upset about his comment. He shook his head. He was setting an excellent example for his students. Here he was insulting the woman in front of the twelve students staring at him.

Way to go Stin. What next?

"How dare you be so rude to me? Who do you think you are, Stin Vanderson?"

Stin raised his hand in defense.

"You're right. I'm sorry Tonia. I didn't mean to insult you in front of my fellow students." He forced a smile. "You said you were looking for Ford, right?"

Tonia's body started to relax.

"Yes. I haven't heard from him lately, have you seen him?"

"If I'm not mistaken, I think he might be in the gym on the other side of the building," Stin said.

"This building has two gyms?" another student asked, this time a female. Tonia glared at the student before her eyes shifted to Stin.

"Thank you." Tonia turned on her heel and strutted out of the door. Stin stared at the curve of her buttocks swaying every which way until she disappeared into the hallway.

Nice

Whoa, where did that come from?

Stin shifted his weight. He didn't have time to deal with stringless one night stands right now. He needed to act like a professional.

"Okay my fellow students, let's take it from the top again…"

"Hey, why did you back off from her Mr. V, you could have really shown her what it's like to disrespect a man." Some of the other male students giggled and laughed while the girls scoffed and rolled their eyes.

"Actually, it was very disrespectful to treat Tonia the way I did. I shouldn't have been so rude to her in front of you guys, and for that, I deeply apologize. It's not nice to be disrespectful to anyone, let alone a woman," Stin explained. *There.* He didn't want them to get the wrong impression about him.

He shouldn't have cared either way considering he would no longer be teaching them within the next two months. Ford would be back to his job as a teacher, and he would officially be the surfer he was always meant to be. But for right now, he didn't need to get into any more trouble than what he just got into a few minutes ago. He wouldn't hear the end of it from his best friend and current boss.

Stin let the thought echo for a few more minutes. He couldn't believe how he ended up being best friends with his boss.

Stranger things had happened.

"Okay, let's take it from the top again," Stin repeated the same instructions as before, paying attention to the students in the back row. He recalled what he wanted to do earlier and searched for the boy—Lex?— throughout the gym.

He'd disappeared again.

What was up with this kid? Stin thought. He continued on with the lesson, keeping a mental note to talk to him after the class was over about walking out during school hours.

And maybe try to figure out what he was hiding in the process…

CHAPTER SEVEN

"Ready?"

"Bring it on."

Ford concentrated on his hand until another fireball appeared. He threw the fireball like a baseball, the ball flying through the air.

Mandy concentrated on the ball and felt the electricity glide from her head down to her arms. The electricity shot out from her fingers on both sides. The fireball inched closer to her. Within seconds, she hit it with the palm of her hand. The electricity caught the ball and threw it across the room. The impact caused the ball to explode in mid-air. It was just enough for the ball to fall to ashes.

"That's good. You did very well," Ford said. He was surprised. Usually, when Ford was with his students, it took them a while to learn such a simple concept. He always thought it was because of their lack of concentration and not being able to focus on the task at hand. There was always some kid who wanted to test his abilities, which meant a full head-on battle. The results weren't usually good for either of them.

This time was different.

He was enjoying himself with her. After a few tense moments of losing her concentration, Mandy was able to focus and use her power to defend herself against him. The feeling was incredible. Now here they were, challenging each other's abilities, trying to figure out who was better.

So far, she was winning.

"You're doing an excellent job I must say. Your powers are getting stronger by the hour. At the rate you're going, you might not need that much training…"

"Which means I could finally get out of here and go back home—wherever home is," Mandy said. Ford saw the huge smile creeping up on Mandy's face. His heart sank. A part of him didn't want her to leave. It was way too dangerous for her to go exploring the world alone with all of this power. She couldn't leave. Not now. It was just too dangerous. By the visit he had with Dr. Madison, he knew he was getting closer to the truth.

He needed that information to protect her.

"Well, let us not get ahead of ourselves Mandy. After all, this is your first day of practice," Ford said.

"But you said I'm better than some of the people you dealt with, right?"

Ford nodded. "Yes, but we still have a long way to go." He paused. "I hate to inform you of this, but I'm afraid you won't be able to go back to the life you once lived. You're an Orman now. Things have changed." Ford saw her smile fade from her lips. Now he felt like a bastard for destroying whatever fantasy she had in her head.

"What do you mean?"

"I mean the island of Truson is your home now. We can't let you go out into the real world with the kind of powers you have. It's too dangerous. It's part of the rules here on the island."

"Oh," Mandy said. Her face dropped. After realizing she wasn't going anywhere, she shrugged. "Oh well, it's no big deal I guess. I don't even remember what home is anyway." Her light green eyes glistened from the dim lighting in the gym.

His abdomen stirred. His alter ego was excited…a little too excited to be exact. He wanted to come out and explore her in ways he could only imagine. He wanted every touch, every kiss, every lick…

His alter ego wanted her more than before…*He* wanted her more than before. His body felt different. This was a new experience for him. He tried to remember the same feelings he had for his wife. He sensed the strong urge to be with her, but it had been awhile since he felt *this* strongly.

"Are we done for today?" Mandy asked.

"Leaving so soon? I thought we were having fun?" he teased, lightening the mood.

"We are, but after the workout I had today, you were right. I need a shower." Mandy smelled her armpits. "I stink."

Ford laughed.

"By all means, take a shower. They are on the other side of the hallway."

"Thanks." Mandy bolted out the door. Ford watched her as she bumped into another female. Mandy apologized to her before she reached her destination. Once Ford saw her brown skin and hazel eyes, he automatically knew who the other woman was. He was happy to say hi, but Tonia had different plans. She wrapped her arms around him and gave him a long peck on the cheek before she stepped back and stared at him.

"I was so worried about you, Ford. I thought you disappeared on me," she said. Tonia was another member of the Truson S.E.T. who also happened to be another good friend of Ford's.

"I don't know whether you've heard the latest news or not—"

"I have. Dr. Madison told me last minute she needed to leave town. She told me it was an emergency but—"

"Wait, Hold on." Ford took a breath and cradled his face in his hands. The gesture ended with his hand massaging his forehead. "You mean to tell me Dr. Madison is out of town again? Does that woman not realize how important this whole training was to me?"

Tonia rubbed Ford's shoulders, but Ford jerked himself away from her.

"Ford, it's okay—"

"No, it isn't Tonia. The whole reason why I decided to give up teaching my fellow students was so I could find out who killed my wife."

"I know Ford, that's why—"

"No, you don't, Tonia. You don't know what it's like to lose someone in your life…not like I lost Roxanne."

Ford turned his back to Tonia. Who was Dr. Madison to take off like this after their conversation this morning? Ten years of searching for answers and now he had to wait until Dr. Madison got back from whatever trip she was taking.

Bullshit.

"Well, you're right. I may not know what it's like to have a spouse, but I certainly know what it's like to lose someone I love, Ford." She placed her hand on his shoulder and jerked him back to face her. "Don't you ever forget that Ford Mayfield. Do you understand?"

He gave himself a few moments to calm down. He shut his eyes and thought about something that made him happy. Images of him and Mandy relaxing on the beaches of Hawaii, being happy caused him to settle his emotions.

"Sorry," he said. "Shouldn't have said it."

Tonia shifted her head, skeptical if she wanted to accept his apology.

"Apology accepted," she finally said. "Are you ready to hear the news I have for you?"

"Yes please."

"Dr. Madison told me to let you know she's on the right track when it comes to finding out who killed Roxanne. She thinks she knows who might have been responsible for Roxanne's death even though she doesn't have proof," Tonia said.

Ford's brow arched.

"Really? Who?"

"Your so-called best friend at the time before you became an Orman—Vernon Stevenson."

Ford couldn't believe what he was hearing. It couldn't have been the same man. He had a sneaking suspicion Vernon wanted Roxanne for himself based on what Roxanne told him the night before their big trip to Hawaii.

"Ford, are you okay?"

The words Roxanne used echoed in his mind. *I think he wants me for himself Ford. I don't trust him.* Now it was starting to make sense to him. He remembered the fight he had with Vernon based on what Roxanne had said, how smug and arrogant he became when Ford confronted him with accusations Roxanne made.

Accusations he didn't want to believe.

"Ford, can you hear me? Talk to me, Ford."

He felt his powers rising. Heat radiated his skin. How could he of all people destroy the one person he loved so much? If this happened to be true, there wasn't going to be anything left of Vernon once Ford got his hands on him.

"Ford, you're scaring me. Talk to me please?" Tonia asked.

"When is she going to get proof?"

Tonia sighed in relief. "I don't know. I guess when she comes back from her trip, she'll start on it again."

"I can't wait that long. If Vernon is the one who killed my wife, I need to stop him before he hurts anyone else," Ford said. "I need to jog Mandy's memory. Maybe I could find someone or something that could make her remember."

"Who's Mandy?"

"Dr. Madison's latest experiment. The whole reason why I'm training Mandy is so that Dr. Madison needed time to find more information about who is responsible for Roxanne's death."

"Do you think they are somehow connected?" Tonia asked.

"I don't know. I can't tell if Lex and Mandy are connected because Mandy has amnesia. She can't even remember her own name," Ford said. His forehead creased. This whole process was starting to get more complicated by the day. If he didn't want to avenge the death of his wife, he would have walked away a long time ago.

Anger rose inside him. He couldn't just stand by and let another day pass without finding Vernon. He needed to be stopped. There was no way Ford was going to wait on this anymore. He wanted proof, and through hell and high water, he was going to get it.

"So, if she can't remember her name, how are you going to prove they are connected?"

"They have to be. When Mandy first woke up from the accident, she had an imprint of what looked to be a wedding ring on her index finger," Ford explained.

"Indicating that she's married?"

Ford nodded.

"Wow. Do you know if her husband contacted her yet?"

Husband. The word sent chills down his spine. How could she have possibly been married to someone like him? Didn't matter. She was here now. He needed to protect her. He couldn't let anything happen to her.

Not now, not ever.

"He doesn't care about anyone but himself," Ford said. He paused when he saw Mandy standing only a few feet away from the entrance. Did she hear the whole conversation between him and Tonia? How long had she been standing there?

Ford took a couple of steps toward Mandy. Mandy moved back.

"Mandy, I can explain…"

"Explain what? That you were somehow using me to find out who killed your wife?"

"I'm sorry Mandy. The truth is I—"

"What Ford? That you couldn't be honest with me? Figures. I should have known something was up when you and Dr. Madison were talking like I wasn't in the room this morning." Mandy waited. "What else have you been hiding from me, huh?"

"Mandy, it's not like that. I don't even know that you're still married. Dr. Madison didn't inform me."

"Well maybe I should talk to Dr. Madison then," Mandy said.

"I'm afraid that's not possible," Tonia piped in.

"Why not?"

"Unfortunately, she's out of town at the moment." Tonia smiled. "But if you like, I'm here to answer whatever questions you need to ask."

"Why? Did Dr. Madison tell you all of my business too?"

"That's enough!" Ford barked. "You're upset about what you've heard, I get it, but you have no reason to take it out on Tonia—"

"I can do whatever I want considering what I just heard. I don't like to be lied to, and I'm damn sure I don't like to be used by someone I could care less about." She turned and paused. "The training is over. I'm leaving this island for good."

No! You can't let her go, it's too dangerous!

Fortunately, Ford didn't have to do much of anything. He watched Tonia call Mandy's name. Mandy didn't respond, causing Tonia to shoot out bits of poison into her back.

"Tonia, no!"

"It's the only way she'll listen. Besides, she was very mean and disrespectful to you and I won't stand for it," Tonia said. After only a few seconds, Mandy was down. Her body shook violently on the floor as Ford raced to her.

"Mandy! Mandy, talk to me please!"

Tonia took her time walking toward Ford and Mandy. Minutes after the incident, Ford saw Lex coming through the door and saw the woman on the ground, having convulsions from the attack.

"What happened to her?" Lex got on his knees and pressed his head to her chest.

Her body couldn't lie still.

"We need to get her back to the lab. She suffered a horrible accident," Ford said. With his arms underneath her back, Ford carried her.

"I'm going with you!" Lex shouted at him.

Ford raced out of the gym in a flash, his mind set on trying to get Mandy healthy again. Sure, he was upset about the argument they had, but it didn't give Tonia permission to go after Mandy the way she had. He needed to talk to her after all of this was over.

He wasn't happy with her at all.

Ford continued to race down the stairs, his thoughts centered on Mandy's recovery. Before Ford managed to reach the double doors of the building, he felt her shaking. It only took him a few seconds to realize she was having a seizure…

Definitely need to talk to Tonia or strangle her, whichever comes first.

***

Tonia stood off to the side while Ford and some white boy she didn't recognize scurried Mandy back to the lab. She could have cared less about her. How dare she talk about Ford in that manner? The accusations were horrendous—Ford using her to get to who killed his wife? She scoffed. It was justified. Tonia always hated the way Ford talked about Roxanne anyway.

To her, it felt like no matter what Roxanne did—sleeping with Ford's ex-best friend, the constant fights they had—Ford always loved her and made excuses for her whenever he could.

And it was that mere thought she hated. That thought always wanted to make her puke. And now? Now she felt the same way about this new girl, Mandy. She didn't like her, especially after she finally connected two and two together when she announced that Vernon Stevenson might be responsible for Roxanne's death. She was the connection.

Or at least Tonia thought she was. Why would Dr. Madison pick Ford out of all people to take care of her? It seemed sort of a coincidence that Ford was chosen out of the five of them. Tonia was more than capable of taking care of Mandy as long as she knew to stay away from Ford. But she wasn't chosen, Ford was.

Why?

Tonia needed to find out. If Ford was in any type of danger, she needed to know about it. Tonia wasn't going to let anyone hurt him, not even this new woman Dr. Madison cooked up to expand the Truson S.E.T. empire. After just meeting her today, Tonia realized how much she despised her. The question was, did she feel guilty about what she'd done?

Yes.

Her first instinct was to protect Ford and no one else. Maybe she shouldn't have put so much poison into her system. She watched Ford check Mandy's pulse before her body shook. Despite how she felt about the woman, she didn't want her to die. Maybe a little poison would have done her some good…Just enough so she would remember what would happen if she ever talked to Ford in a manner Tonia didn't like. Tonia smiled. She loved punishment, not death.

Death was not in her vocabulary unless she was attacked by an enemy of course.

Now onto pressing matters…

Tonia dug into her pocket for her cell. When she grabbed it, she scrolled through her contact list. She punched in the numbers and called Dr. Madison in every place she thought she could be—Florida, California, New York, Las Vegas…

Nothing.

How could a woman just disappear like that without an explanation? Why did she have to leave Tonia with the responsibility of telling Ford what she *possibly* knew? Would Dr. Madison just stay on the island for one second so she could help Ford with this investigation?

Tonia shook her head. Whatever. She didn't have time for this. She needed to pretend to be concerned about what happened to Mandy. If she didn't, she knew Ford would never forgive her. She couldn't have that on her conscience.

She was about to call another number to see if she could contact Dr. Madison when the creak of the gym door distracted her. She started to get her hopes up about Ford coming back and telling her Mandy was going to be okay.

"Have you seen anyone in here?"

Her heart sank. Stin was the last person she wanted to see.

"Why are you asking? I'm pretty sure Ford doesn't need your company right now."

Stin's eyebrows creased. He pointed his finger at her.

"Are you always such a bitch or are you just having a bad day?"

She could feel the anger rising in her body again. She walked up to Stin and without thinking about the consequences of her actions, slapped him in his face. Stin wailed in pain as the poison began to invade his skin.

"I didn't mean to do that. I'm so sorry," Tonia said.

"Yes, you did! You did it on purpose." He put his hand on the poison and felt the green liquid oozing down his cheek.

"No don't—"

It was too late. The poison was already on his fingers. Pretty soon, it would spread all over. As much as she hated the guy, she didn't want him to die. She put her hands on her face.

"Okay, you just need some Binosil. But first, we need to get you to the bathroom." She tried to touch him, but he jerked his arm away and sprinted to the bathroom. Tonia followed behind and watched him douse himself with warm water. She tried to volunteer her help, but Stin refused to let her near him.

"Stand back! I don't want you to make it any worse than you already have."

"I'm trying to help you," Tonia said. "The poison is gone already. I'm not going to hurt you again."

"Stand back!"

Tonia stood back and watched him pour water on his face. It didn't take long for the guilt to settle in about her reaction to the whole situation.

"Well I'm sorry my poison landed on you, but you were the one who called me a bitch. Don't you think you were disrespectful when you said that to me?"

Stin stuck his head out from under the sink and ran his fingers through his hair. "I wasn't trying to be disrespectful to you—I—just—"

She could see the inflammation of his cheekbones slowly revealing the inside of his skull. *Not good,* she thought. She needed the Binosil. The question was how was she going to get to the lab and make it back in time? Stin let out a huge muffled sound and Tonia watched him stampede the hallway like an elephant before disappearing down the stairs.

He's transforming. Maybe all the water plus the powers that he had were enough to get rid of the poison for good.

Tonia reassured herself everything was going to be okay. All she needed was to get inside the lab, get some Binosil, find Stin and try to inject it so the poison didn't take his life. She wasn't sure if her key card would get her into the lab. She tried to think of one other person besides Dr. Madison who might have the keycard.

She swore.

Ford had it, but he was attending to Mandy's needs at the moment all because of her attempt to save someone she might have a future with.

Just great Tonia, what else could go wrong today?

Tonia didn't have time to answer the question as she fled out the door to find him.

CHAPTER EIGHT

Lex watched as Ford laid Mandy down on the bed and checked her pulse. She was still alive despite the poison. Lex couldn't take his eyes off of Ford as he used his keycard to open the cabinet doors a couple of feet away from the lab. He grabbed a small bottle and a needle and shut the door.

"What do you think you're doing?" Lex barked.

"Saving her life." Ford injected the clear liquid into the syringe and threw the bottle to the other side of the room. Before he could insert the fluid into her veins, Lex grabbed his arms.

"I refuse to let you do it. I won't let you kill her," he said.

"If I don't inject this drug into her within the next few minutes, she will die." They stared at each other for a few more seconds before Lex pulled his hand away. Ford injected the Binosil into her veins and waited. He stared at his watch. A whole ten minutes passed before Mandy's body calmed down. Lex waited for any sign of movement. He knew what he was going to do to Ford if she didn't move…

Lex saw a flicker of her eyelids before they opened up fully. He was relieved to see a beautiful pair of green eyes staring back at him. Ever since his dad introduced him to her, he always thought they were the perfect couple…That was before he found out what was really going on. He didn't want to admit it, but he knew what his dad was capable of.

He'd had to kill her. At the time, it was the only way he was able to get the money he needed to keep the roof over their heads until Mandy's parents decided to block Vernon from the will. That's when his dad thought up the plan to kill Ford.

If Lex killed Ford, they would be able to regain the monetary compensation they deserved, and they could go back to the way things were before. The problem was, he never realized his stepmother was still alive—until now. For the last couple of days, his father had lied and told him there was a car accident causing them to veer off the road and into the freezing waters off Alaska. His father went on to say he was lucky to be alive based on his swimming skills but said it was already too late for Mandy—she died as soon as she hit the water.

Or so he thought.

"Who are you?" Ford asked.

Lex couldn't take his eyes off of the woman. The woman—the same woman he believed was his stepmother—seemed unresponsive to the situation.

"I asked you a question."

"The name's Lex," he said. After hearing about what happened between Ford and his father, the last thing the man needed from him was an explanation.

"Lex who? Who are you and why are you hanging around Mandy?"

When Lex decided to stay put and not give Ford the attention he wanted, Ford grabbed him by his shirt and lifted him to his height. His feet dangled a few inches from the floor. "Did you hear what I just said?"

The whole thing should have frightened him. Any ordinary teenage boy probably would have been considering how much strength Ford had. Not Lex. He wasn't intimidated in the least. He closed his eyes and concentrated, sending signals of his powers through his body. Lex felt Ford's arm shake as Lex's body turned into boulders.

Ford let go of Lex's neck before the full transition took effect. Lex watched Ford take a couple of steps back before he took a stance. Ford wanted to challenge him, he could tell by the look on his face. *No worries, I can beat him. There's no way he could have the same type of powers I have. Bring it on.*

It didn't take long for Lex to fully transform into his true alter ego. With boulders the size of small mountains, he flexed his muscles and took a stance of his own. He was prepared for anything that stood in his way. Screw the fact Ford would already be dead once he struck. He lived for the thrill of seeing his enemies suffer before sucking the life out of them.

This was going to be fun.

Ford Mayfield kept his stance with his hands out in front of him, ready for an attack. They continued to lock eyes with anticipation, each one waiting to see which one would strike first. Lex scoffed. Ford wanted him to strike.

What a coward.

Lex raised his right arm and opened his palm. Inside he held a ten-inch boulder, one that could easily roll off a limb if given the strength. Lex swung back his arm and…

"Stop!" a voice cried. "No Lex!"

Lex and Ford focused on her. Both of them ran to her bedside.

"Mandy?" Ford took a breath. "How are you feeling?" Ford gently brushed his thumb on her forehead. "Are you okay?"

"Yes. Surprisingly, Tonia didn't do any major damage to me—at least I hope she didn't. Is there…" She stopped to catch her breath.

"…Someone in the building who could check your vitals?" Ford finished. "We have a small number of doctors on call. I have arranged for one to check on you. He should be here any minute."

Good. Lex wanted to say the comment out loud, but since his body was made out of boulders, he couldn't speak…one of his many flaws he could never master.

"Are you hurt anywhere? Do you need anything?" Mandy's eyes drifted to Lex. He knew he was on the right track. He'd heard her call his name. She knew exactly who he was.

So many questions…

"Is he okay?" she asked. "He doesn't seem like it."

Lex nodded yes, hoping to answer her question. He needed to turn back into his human form. The only way he could do that was if he went back into the water and transitioned from boulder machine to orca and then back to his human form again. Since he used all of his skin and bones to outstretch himself to fit his boulder form, he needed to use his alter ego to calm himself down and heal his body before he decided to go human again.

The downsides to being a Transforment.

"I'm pretty sure he's fine but speaking of that…" Ford trailed off and briefly pointed the finger at him before shifting his gaze back to Mandy. "Do you recognize him? I seem to recall you saying his name during our disagreement." Lex shifted his head toward Mandy. He didn't remember a time when she saw him transform into the hard-knocking man she saw before her. The whole image must have frightened her.

"Yes…Yes, I remember him. He—he meant something to me. I don't know why considering how he looks. I don't remember seeing him in this form, but I did see him before he transformed into what he is now…" She took a couple of deep breaths.

"So, you know him?" Ford asked. Lex wanted nothing more than to respond to the statement but couldn't. He had so many mixed emotions about her but so many questions as well. A part of him was angry at her for staying away so long. Why didn't she come back home to his father and him? If she was mad at them, why didn't she say anything? At the same time, he remembered what his dad said about the car accident. Was she somehow afraid to go back home?

"Yes…I—I think I remember him—he's my—son"

Can't remember who I am His mind screamed.

Lex's heart thumped inside his chest. He needed to get out of here before the situation got any worse. The fear of his secret identity being revealed caused him to think about the last time he received a call from his father. His once brilliant plan of taking down his dad's worst enemy was now falling to pieces. He needed to go back to his other form before she spilled the truth.

"Your son??? You have a son?" Ford asked.

Lex couldn't take it anymore. He needed air. He took one final look at his stepmother before he disappeared out of the room and searched for the nearest exit. He started to panic when he saw Stin coming from the opposite direction followed by the woman who interrupted his class earlier in the day. Lex had forgotten her name, but it didn't matter. He just wanted to disappear.

All because he wanted to prove a point to his dad.

He then thought about the cell he'd given Stin earlier in the day. He swore. If Stin ever called the number, the whole plan was over, and everyone would know exactly who he was. Vernon had trusted him with one responsibility—killing Ford, and he already failed.

Plan A had officially gone out the window.

No worries. There had to be other ways to kill Ford. All he had to do was think of another plan that could possibly work in his favor. But first, he had to turn back into his other form, so his body could fully heal. He just prayed Mandy didn't give away his secret in the process.

***

With his face and body somehow healing from the repulsive poison Tonia had slapped into him, Stin decided he needed to talk to Ford alone. Shortly after the little incident with Tonia, he managed to squeeze some time in to check Lex's cell and trace the calls he'd been receiving since yesterday. Only one name popped up, but this name was one that made him want to punch a wall in.

Vernon Stevenson.

Even though he had no proof he did it, Stin was suspicious about him as an Orman.

He did a massive number on Ford once he found out Vernon wanted his wife to himself. When he couldn't have her, he decided to make Ford suffer by killing his wife. Of all the rules on the island of Truson, killing humans as well as members of their own were definitely the biggest ones. There was no way Vernon could survive within the team after that. He'd killed people that meant so much to both of them.

He needed to pay.

Yet before he could face any punishment for what he had done, Vernon fled like the coward he was. Ever since then, they were dead on his trail. Unfortunately, Vernon was one of those Ormans who knew how to disappear. No matter how close they came to finding him, they came up empty.

Until today.

All he needed was for Ford to be alone for the next few minutes so he could relay the information to him. Stin thought it would be possible until—

"Stin! Stin, wait! I'm sorry, I didn't mean it. I just want to check and see if you're okay."

"Tonia, I'm really not in the mood right now. I have a very important message I need to deliver to Ford. The last thing I need is for you to keep stalking me so back off."

"But I—"

"Back off!" Stin yelled.

The anger in his voice sent Tonia back a few inches, but she bounced back quickly. "I was only trying to help you out. Since you don't want my help, I suggest it would be best if you just stay the hell away from me."

"Fine by me," Stin said, shrugging his shoulders. The yelling match fizzled when they saw a tall short-haired man enter the room. Both of them stepped forward to follow the doctor but then stepped back the moment they realized they had to make contact with each other. *Screw this,* Stin thought. He got in front of Tonia and managed to be in time for the conversation. Ford and the doctor greeted each other before he got down to business.

"Based on the information you told me, I believe she suffered or inhaled some type of poison, is that correct?"

"Yes," Ford replied. "She took a lot of it. She started having multiple seizures on our trip to the lab. I gave her a dose of Binosil to relieve some of the pain she might have experienced during the seizure, and her seizures stopped."

"Ummm, interesting. It's amazing what Dr. Madison does with all of those chemicals. I have to admit she was a real genius when it came to situations like these," the doctor said. The doctor scribbled some notes down on a piece of paper. "Do you know what kind of poison it is?"

"It's called camel poison," Tonia said. All eyes focused on her. Though she was thrown off by the attention, she continued. "It's a poison I use to paralyze and kill my enemies. A small dosage could kill an Orman within twenty-four hours."

The doctor lifted a brow.

"And humans?"

Tonia's eyes landed on the floor.

"Less than that," was all she could mutter. She was too ashamed to stare at the one person whom she'd adored ever since she landed on the island.

"She's not human," Ford said. "Dr. Madison injected the Animan Three-Hundred into her system not long after her death."

Stin heard Tonia give out an exhale. She was way too lucky when it came to situations like this. She needed to be held accountable for her actions.

She needed to be punished. Period.

"Well, that's somewhat good."

"What do you mean somewhat good?" Mandy asked. "Is the poison still in me or not?"

The doctor sighed.

"Yes. Once you have poison in your system, it's up to us to figure out what kind of poison it is and how best to treat it, so it doesn't do any major damage to your organs. In this case, we already know you have camal poison, so I need to find out more information about it. I'm hoping Ms.

Tonia will assist me with whatever I need so I can make this patient feel better."

"She'll be more than happy to do it," both men said. They exchanged glances between them and Tonia before they shifted back to the doc.

"Good. This might take a while, so you're more than welcome to go out and get some fresh air." The doctor took out his stethoscope and listened to Mandy's heart.

"I need to do an X-ray on her heart. Would you mind giving us a few minutes?"

"I can wait a few minutes," Ford replied. Stin stepped up.

"We'll be back. There's something I need to discuss with Ford anyway."

Ford raised a brow. Stin could tell he wanted to argue with him but decided against it.

"Go, Ford. I'll be okay. The doctor is not going to leave my side. Besides, there's security everywhere. If something's wrong, I'm sure they are going to be able to come to my aid."

"She's right Ford. You've been by her side for the last three days. It's time you took a break man. We need to catch up on a lot of things," Stin said. He gave him one good tap on the shoulder. "C'mon, why don't we go get something to eat and chill out on the island for a while?" Stin sensed Ford's hesitation about leaving Mandy alone but saw by the expression on his face Stin was winning.

"I'll be back as soon as I can."

"Take your time," Mandy said.

Ford went back to Mandy's bed and kissed her on the forehead. Stin saw the vast grimace Tonia had on her face and smiled. *Totally enjoying the despair.*

Ford and Stin shut the door behind them and proceeded down the hallway. It had been a while since they had some breathing room to sit down and chat about things.

"So, what were you going to tell me in there? I was hoping it was information on who murdered Roxanne."

"Why? Did someone tell you something about it already?" Stin asked, concerned he might have been wasting his time.

"I hope not, but if you're here telling me Dr. Madison is somewhere on vacation and that Vernon might possibly be the killer, I've already made arrangements to set him on fire when I see him."

"And I'll be your trusty sidekick every step of the way," Stin said, extending his arms into the air. "Remember we are each other's strengths as well as our weaknesses."

"I agree," Ford said. "Is that what you wanted to tell me or do you have something else for me to see?"

"It's something similar to that. There's something I found out that's gonna pique your interest. When I saw it, I wanted to know more."

"What is it?" Ford asked.

Tell him before he starts to lose interest. "The other day, I had a student who was using a cell during school hours. Normally, I wouldn't go through people's private stuff, but something told me to give it a shot, so I did."

Ford leaned forward. "What did you find?"

"I think Vernon and this student are related. If they are, I was wondering if you wanted me to keep an eye on him, in case he makes any sudden moves," Stin said.

He heard Ford clicking down on the arrow key and stopped. A flash of orange light appeared. He was upset. Majority of the time, he was calm and rational. The name popped up on the screen. Ford's eyes grew darker.

"This would be the second time his name has been mentioned today, and I'm getting really tired of it. Who had the cellphone?"

"His name is Lex. I don't know if you've heard of him or not…"

"Yes, I have. I just saw him a few minutes ago. I don't know if you were paying attention, but he was the young man strutting out of the hospital in boulders. Apparently, he's an Orman too."

The question was how? For the longest time, Stin and the others thought they were the only Ormans that existed on the island. Now that had officially changed. Stin saved the thought in the back of his mind.

"What did he want?" Stin asked.

"To see Mandy. She called him her son. Apparently, she and Vernon had a son together."

"She and Vernon? Wait, wait a minute." Stin paused. "You mean to tell me the woman you have been training had a son with a man we both suspect is responsible for your wife's death?

"Yes." Silence. "I started piecing things together after Tonia told me of Dr. Madison's confession about

Vernon's connection to Roxanne's death. I had a feeling Mandy and Vernon were somehow connected. But now I know the truth—They were married and had a son together."

"So, she's married to him?"

"Afraid so," Ford replied. "A couple of days ago, I saw an imprint of what looked to be a wedding ring on her left index finger." As they approached the stairway, they remained silent. It was only when they bounded toward the end of the stairwell that they started talking again.

"Before we go any farther, let's look at what's in front of us right now. We now know Mandy is the woman who may be married to the man who's responsible for killing your wife."

Ford nodded.

"Then based on the information I received from Lex's phone, Lex is a student who may possibly be Mandy and Vernon's son?"

Ford felt something growing inside his chest. He didn't want to think about those two being married, let alone having a teenage son. Mandy had a life and a family to go back home to. Ford knew the whole husband thing was going to go out the window once he found proof about Vernon killing Roxanne. He couldn't help but wonder where her life was going to end up after the battle was over.

"What's our next move?" Stin asked. They both stopped and stared at the place labeled "Nise's Bar and Grill" in big fancy cursive letters and flashing neon lights.

"Let's just figure that out once we get inside, shall we?"

CHAPTER NINE

Despite the island being so isolated from the rest of the world, Nise's Bar and Grill still remained a place to go whenever the Truson S.E.T. wanted to kick back and relax—when they needed a break from saving the world. Ford and Stin made themselves comfortable by easing onto the stools. After wiping off a couple of glasses, Nise finally turned and greeted them with a warm smile.

"Well if it isn't my two favorite people strolling into the bar."

"Is that your best joke? If it is, it sucks," Stin replied. Ford snorted.

"No, it's not my best joke *Stin,* but if you don't want me to give you a compliment, why don't I insult you instead weenie man."

Ford started chuckling.

"Don't call me that, okay? My boy's right here."

Ford gave him a firm pat on the shoulder.

"You don't have to worry about that, dude. Nise told me all about it after it happened."

Stin shifted his weight and leaned forward. "You told him what happened? How could you do that to me? I thought we could at least be friends Nise." Nise lifted her hand and slapped him on the cheek.

"We are friends, darlin'. You see, you thought you were going to sleep with me and get away with it."

"No, I didn't," Stin lied. "I wanted someone to cuddle with—"

"You wanted someone to screw, Stin. You're a player. You like to run game on all sorts of women. You thought you were gonna get away with it when it came to me, but I had different plans," Nise said.

"Plans like what?"

Nise stood up from the bar. "Since I knew you were going to tell all of your so-called friends about your sex life, I decided to beat you to the punch. I told all of your friends about our one-night stand."

Stin's mouth dropped.

Ford's chuckles became a full-blown laugh once he saw the expression on Stin's face.

"What? Got nothing to say weenie-man?"

Stin's chair scooted against the floor as he rose to his feet and pointed his finger at her.

"Don't you call me that anymore. I mean it. I'll make sure the whole island knows what type of woman you are," Stin said. Anger rose in his voice. Ford could see his skin growing pale. His laughter slowed down. As much as he enjoyed Nise getting Stin all riled up, he needed to stop the conversation before Stin did something he regretted.

"As much as I love the conversation here, I'm quite thirsty. You got anything to drink?"

"Sure do, hot shot," Nise said. She winked. "What would you like?"

"The best drink you can find." Ford felt guilty about drinking alcohol considering the reaction his alter ego had whenever he drank too much. He thought about the days when he used to drink straight out of the bottle. His alter ego would have a fit, and he would spend the rest of his day puking out what was left from the night before. He used Roxanne's death as an excuse to drink.

He had to make a choice—move on and try to find who was responsible for killing his wife or die another miserable death, never to return to Earth again, Orman or otherwise. After one more night of endless drinking, he decided to channel his attention toward finding out who was responsible for his wife's death.

So far it worked.

"All right. What about you Stin?" Nise asked.

Stin scoffed.

"Just give me what he's having, okay?"

"Coming right up doll." She jotted down some notes then left the bar, leaving them alone.

"Can you believe her? How dare she embarrass me like that? I'm Stin Vanderson. She should show me some respect dammit, I'm one of her best-paying customers here!"

Ford shook his head.

"What? Stop shaking your head at me like that. You know it's true."

"Stin, calm down. If you get too riled up, your powers are going to come to the surface. You don't want to cause a scene here." Stin stared at the row of glasses in front of him. He knew Ford was right. This place happened to be the only place where humans and Ormans hung out together. If one of the Ormans thought about causing a scene, all hell would break loose. The Truson Super Elite Team was a secret society no one knew about except them and maybe a few of their enemies. It needed to stay that way.

"You're right, man. You're right." Nise came back with two glasses of bourbon.

"If you guys need anything else just holler."

"Thanks, Nise," Ford called after she left the bar to service another customer.

Stin snorted. "How've you been doing man? You know, with the holiday and all?" Memories flooded through Ford's brain again. He felt a vast sting in his chest. *Just when I was having a great time.*

"I'm fine." Ford took a huge gulp from his glass. "Besides, we're supposed to be talking about Lex, remember?"

"I know, but this is a hard holiday for you. Here we are celebrating the nation's independence, and here you are upset about your wife being killed. Are you okay?"

"I was until you mentioned it. Thanks a lot, friend," Ford said. He took another swig and slammed the glass down on the table. "Nise, another glass please."

"Whoa! Hey man, I didn't want you to go all crazy with the drinks dude."

"Stin, can we just get to the point, please? I would really like to go back to the lab to check on Mandy." Stin took a couple of swallows before he spoke.

"You know, I didn't think it would happen, but after ten years of being alone, I think it finally has."

"What?"

"You're officially moving on my friend," Stin said.

"What are you talking about?" Ford leaned his head to the side, wondering if he was going to hug him or slug him within the next few minutes.

"Oh c'mon Ford, I'm not an idiot. I know it when I see it, dude. It was the same kind of look you had when you and Roxanne were together. You two—" He nodded. "It was forever dude. Everyone knew it."

"Stin, I didn't become an Orman until after the Jet Ski explosion. You never met her."

"I didn't need to meet her to know you were in love with her. Hell, you've been searching for ten years trying to figure out who was responsible for her death. If that's not love, then I don't know what is." Silence fell between them before Stin volunteered to start again. "I just wanted to know how you were doing, that's all."

"How do you think I'm doing? I just found out the woman I've rescued is married to my former best friend who tried to seduce my wife. When he didn't succeed, he decided to blow us up in Hawaii—"

"Okay—"

"Then today, I found out my supportive partner who dragged me into the situation in the first place decides to flee town but not before leaving a message to one of the members stating that she thinks Vernon is responsible for my wife's death…without any proof!"

"Dude, I get—"

"Then, my best friend tells me some kid—Lex—the same kid who tried to kill me a couple of hours ago—might possibly be the son of a killer. Are you really sure you want to ask me how I'm doing?"

Stin held his hands up.

"You're right. Besides, I wanted us to come here, talk about what I found, and be done with it. I just wanted us to have a good time since we haven't talked in a while." Ford picked up the glass. Another sting of bourbon shot down his throat. He ordered Nise back to the bar for another.

"A bit of advice—If you want us to have a good time, stop talking about Roxanne's death."

"Got it," Stin said. He did a thumbs up. "Anniversary of your and Roxanne's death banished."

"Fantastic." Ford focused on the screen. His weight shifted when he saw what looked to be Mandy shaking her long curly red hair, running to the water. His insides ached. He felt the tension under his abdomen. His alter ego hurt ever since that day they swam together. No…it was before that…before he even knew her name. Ever since he saw her, all he wanted to do was kiss her, lick her, taste her…

Be inside her…

He was about to get out of his seat to see if she had disappeared when he realized it was a different woman on the TV screen. Ford snorted. He needed to stop thinking about her that way. He was here to get information about his wife's death.

She'll always be your first.

"So, does this mean you're finally starting to move on?" Stin asked, breaking his thoughts.

"What?"

"Dude, I've seen your reaction to Mandy. You're attracted to her." Ford raised a brow.

"Really? And how do you know that, huh? Have you been stalking my every move?"

"No, I don't have time for that, remember? I'm still teaching your wonderful class," Stin said. A small ache filled Ford's chest. He missed teaching his students.

"How long is it going to be before you start teaching again?"

Ford calculated the weeks in his head. Had it been three days already? It didn't feel like it to him. He had been scrambling back and forth between protecting Mandy and that he had somehow managed to let the days slip away from him…something that generally wouldn't happen if he was creating lesson plans and activities for his students. He was always prepared no matter what circumstances arose. But lately, he had to admit he wasn't exactly on top of his game.

"In six months. The deal was to teach Mandy everything about controlling her powers. I'm also teaching her the kind of powers we use to defend ourselves against any enemies, but considering what happened today, I don't think it's going to be possible." Ford paused. Thoughts of Tonia throwing the horrible poison at Mandy flooded his mind. "At least not right away."

"I'm pretty sure you'll get there, dude." Stin took another swig. "Are you going to bang her before you let her go?"

Ford grunted. "What did I just tell you? She's *married*, Stin."

"All the more reason to sleep with her." Stin grabbed the glass. "Think about it man, you haven't had sex with anyone in the last few years. You used to be like me—after Roxanne died, you just slept with any woman you saw with no strings attached." Ford cringed at his words. Though it was true he did sleep with any woman he wanted, he was really trying to fill a void left after the accident.

"I regret sleeping with those women. Unlike you, I don't really like having one-night stands." Ford caught a glimpse of Nise as she took a towel and started wiping off the counter.

"Oh c'mon Ford, having one-night stands is a way of living. There are no strings, no promises of commitment, nothing. You two just get whatever physical attraction you have out of your system and move on."

Ford stared at Nise. She shook her head.

"It's amazing you're still treating women like garbage even after all the damage I've done to you," Nise said. She passed them another glass of bourbon.

"Hey, stay out of this, will you? I'm talking to my best friend here."

"Who really doesn't want your advice on women? Can't you see he's getting annoyed? He doesn't want it."

Ford held his hands in mid-air. "It's all right, Nise." Ford patted Stin on the back. "I know he means well."

"Yeah, he knows it." Stin pointed his thumb at Ford, then directed his finger at Nise. "If you keep up with all of these comments about me, I'm afraid I might have no other choice but to stop being your most valuable customer."

Nise rolled her eyes.

"Whatever you say Stin." She walked to the other side of the room. Stin gave a silent nod before he focused his attention on Ford.

"So, what do you say? You think you could go for it? We all know you want her."

Ford grimaced. The only person who was really paying attention to his situation was Stin. Nobody else would have cared.

"No, you are the only person who is pressing the issue." Memories of her physical features came to his mind again. Ford blocked them out by trying to picture Mandy and Vernon together, enjoying things like a typical married couple would enjoy—a trip to the park, kayaking in a river…

Having sex in a bedroom…

Pain circulated through Ford's hand as shards of glass flew from his fist. The thought of Vernon's hands touching her in that way, knowing that he might have been responsible for murdering Mandy, sparked a fuse inside him.

He needed to protect her.

"Just one final comment and then I won't talk about it anymore—Scout's honor."

Ford exhaled and buried his face in his hands. Why were they best friends again? Before Ford protested, he decided to let Stin get whatever he needed to say out so he could finish his drink and walk back to the lab. "I haven't seen you happy in a long while. You should think about it before you completely dismiss the idea." Stin swallowed his bourbon in one gulp, put the money on the table, and exited the bar.

"Where are you going now?"

"Surfing. I need to burn off some of this energy. Plus, I don't want to get too drunk. We all know what happens when we do."

"That's it? I thought we were going to talk about what you found." Stin stared at the ceiling.

"Right." He dug into his pockets and tossed the cell at Ford. "You can search through that. I want it back though. Can't let Lex suspect anything yet, it'll blow our cover."

Ford nodded.

Stin disappeared into the night, the door slamming behind him. Ford snorted. So much for hanging out with his best bud. He went to the contacts page and scrolled down the list. Ford noticed the name 'dad' programmed into Lex's phone and dialed the number.

His phone beeped.

Ford searched the phone again and saw DAD pop up on his cell. Ford clicked over. This was going to be interesting..

***

Begging. Pleading. *Please stop*, a gruff voice.

You don't love me. You never have. A hit across the face. A body slamming itself on top of the table. *Please stop. I love you, please stop.* Laughter filled the air.

Please stop.

Mandy's eyes flew open. Pain burst in her chest. Blood rushed to her ears. *What was that?* It had to be a bad dream. She turned her head. The clock was in the same spot as before although Mandy felt somewhat different.

This had to be the same place as before, right?

"It's about time you woke up." The voice sounded familiar. Mandy shut her eyes and tried to picture it in her head. Memories of past nightmares crept in, causing her to lose her concentration. "You don't have to worry this time, I'm not going to inject you with my poison again. I thought we could talk woman-to-woman since Ford and Stin aren't here."

Poison? Of course, that's how she landed here in the first place.

"I thought they kicked you out?" Mandy said. "Ford wants you to stay away from me."

Heels clicked against the floor as the dark-skinned woman paced around her bed.

"Well, Ford and Stin tell me a lot of things, but sometimes it's just best for me not to listen."

"I bet that's how you always are, aren't you?" Mandy shifted her weight and sat up. "Always doing whatever you want despite what people tell you." The woman stopped pacing.

"Stop pretending you know everything about me, Mandy. You know nothing."

"I know you have a crush on Ford." Mandy shifted the covers before making eye contact again. "It was obvious."

Tonia stepped toward her. Fear escalated in her body, but she didn't flinch. *If she attacks me again, I'll electrocute her ass.*

Luckily, Tonia stopped herself. "I don't know who you think you are, but you need to cut it out before I put my poison in you again." She leaned in and smiled. "We don't want that, do we?" Mandy smiled back before it quickly faded.

"Why don't you tell me why you're here so I can go back to sleep?" Mandy asked. Tonia snorted at Mandy's comment.

Seriously, what is wrong with this woman?

Tonia put her hands at her sides and started pacing again. "What's—" She stopped. She shook her head and started again. "I'm sorry, you have amnesia, right?"

"How did—"

"Doesn't matter." Tonia paused. "I think it's fascinating Ford is keeping secrets from you. No worries. I'll be able to tell you everything he's been keeping from you." She pulled out a chair, plopped down and straddled her legs on top of the bed. Mandy replayed what Tonia said in her mind. She didn't have time for silly games.

"I'm not quite sure I want to hear this—"

"—You don't want to hear you have a husband?" Tonia interrupted.

"I already know that." Tonia shrugged.

"It's unfortunate you're married to someone Ford is not particularly fond of." Tonia paused. Her eyes flashed from Mandy's light pale face to her unpolished toes. "That's right. I bet you don't even remember how you got here, do you?" Tonia waited for Mandy to respond. She felt too tired to argue. A massive wave of fatigue took over her body.

"I remember you shooting me with your poison and nearly killing me." Tonia smiled.

"I did do that, didn't I?" The smile dropped. "I do apologize for putting too much poison in you. If you were human, you would have probably been dead within a matter of minutes."

"Interesting. How did you know I was married?" Mandy asked.

"Not only do I know you are married, but I also know you are married to a killer. How does it feel to know you are married to the same person who killed you?" Mandy's pulse raced. She couldn't be married to a killer. Who wouldn't know they were married to one?

"You're lying—"

"Am I?" Tonia paused. "As the newest member of our team, I'm surprised you don't know one of our many talents. We can read each other's minds. It's a defense mechanism in case one of us gets in trouble." Unfortunately for Ford, I can see his thoughts…especially when it comes to you."

"That still doesn't explain what you want from me. I would really appreciate it if you would just leave me be.

I'm exhausted after the day I had," Mandy said. She needed to process her thoughts. *Married?* If she was married, then who was she married to? Mandy thought about what Tonia noted earlier.

Was she married to the same person she had nightmares about? Even though she knew Lex looked familiar, she had no memories of giving birth or even images of him as a little boy. All she knew was she didn't want Ford or anyone else to hurt him. Lex was just a child after all.

The question was why? Why was she willing to risk everything to save the kid?

"Look, I'm not here to make your life any more miserable than it is now. That mission has already been accomplished." Tonia gave out a quick smile before she continued. "I just need you to stop and think about one thing before you do anything else."

"Yeah, what's that?"

"Stay away from Ford. Since you're married to someone who could possibly kill us all including Ford, don't you think it would be best if you stayed away from him?" Tonia asked.

Mandy couldn't really process much of anything after that. None of this made any sense. Married? If she were married, wouldn't her husband be worried about her?

Too many questions. Not enough answers.

She needed to see Ford. She was surprised he hadn't returned from his trip with his other friend. Where was he?

Tonia got up from her chair and fixed her outfit. The two women stared at each other in silence. Mandy scoffed.

How desperate was Tonia to get Ford? She had to admit the guy was gorgeous. She hadn't seen a man as handsome as he was for as long as she remembered.

"Very desperate," Tonia replied, answering her question. She shrugged. "Well, I'll let you think about it. Hopefully, you'll agree to stay away from Ford. Have a good night's rest."

She closed the door behind her and left Mandy alone with her thoughts…

CHAPTER TEN

He needed to call his dad.

Lex came out from the water and shook himself off. He knew he was in a lot of trouble because of the whole cellphone situation. If nothing improved within the next few days, his dad would be pissed and kick him out with nowhere to go and nothing to take with him. He sighed. In some ways, that was what he really wanted—freedom. He was sick and tired of "working" for his dad.

Usually, the task would be minor…him getting involved in something that was less dangerous like helping Samuel out with the Transforments, which he always hated because they somehow made fun of his skin color. As a baby, he was diagnosed with albinism. He always hated the sun because of how it felt on his skin, so he decided the best remedy for that was to be in orca form for the majority of the day.

That worked only when he wasn't doing favors for his father. He hated doing favors for anyone. He had to admit this was the first time his father had ever asked him to kill anyone. He had officially failed that on the first day of school. He shrugged. Too much has happened now. That plan had gone out the window when he saw his stepmother alive and well.

He needed his cell to figure out plan B. Now that Mandy was alive and well, he didn't know what to do next. *Protect her,* he thought. *She needs protection.*

Lex played the image of seeing her in bed. She had to be in some sort of trouble. She was in a hospital bed for Christ sakes! What was the matter with him? She needed his protection from the Truson S.E.T., especially from the evil dark-skinned bitch Tonia. He didn't trust her when it came to Mandy, and he had proof of that by the argument he heard raging outside the door between her, Ford and Mandy. While it was great Ford took Mandy back to the lab when he did, he was still unsure of whether he should trust him or not.

Hence, the phone situation.

What time is it? He knew school had let out, but he needed to at least find one of his friends so he could use a cell.

Lex saw what looked to be a woman jogging in the opposite direction. He sprinted to her, hoping she wouldn't turn away. She didn't. Once he got close enough, he realized the woman he sought was the same woman who nearly killed his stepmother.

"Hey, are you all right?" The woman stopped jogging and stared directly at him. He felt his body stretching to its core. He felt his alter ego ripping inside him. He took a deep breath, putting his alter ego in check before he approached her.

"Do you have your cellphone on you? I need to call someone."

Voices escalated outside as a group of teenagers glared at Tonia.

"Yo Tonia, you look hot!"

"The more I see you, the more I want to eat you my dear!"

A burst of laughter echoed throughout the night sky. Lex saw Tonia's eyes flash from light brown to dark green before she put her hands on her hips and turned.

"If you boys don't stop what you're doing right now, you are going to have a very rude awakening."

One of the boys threw his arms out. "Oh yeah? What are you going to do to me, huh? Throw me in the fucking ocean?"

"Enough!" Lex shouted. "Teven and Jamie, stop it!"

They both looked at each other in shock.

"I think we have a new development, Jamie." Teven put his hand behind his ear and inched toward Jamie who seemed to be enjoying the scenario.

"Oh yeah, what's that Teven?"

"I think Lex is a big fat marshmallow and a coward because he's defending a crazy psychopath."

Another burst of laughter. Lex put his arm out, blocking Tonia from reaching them. Though he'd never seen it for himself, he knew she was more than capable of handling the situation alone. He couldn't have that. She already hurt one person he genuinely cared about, he wasn't going to risk losing any more.

No matter how much they deserved it.

"You can't hurt them, they're my friends. Tell you what? I'll handle them. Why don't you go do whatever it was you were doing," Lex said.

"Didn't you want to use my cell?"

Lex shook his head no. He needed to be alone with his friends before they started something they would eventually regret. Lex greeted his friends and turned them around in the opposite direction. Teven and Jamie laughed at the whole situation.

"Did you see the expression on her face? Hilarious!" Teven said.

"Oh God, I wish Mr. Vanderson was here to see that one," Jamie replied. Lex slapped them both on their heads.

"Are you guys stupid? You can't go around making jokes like that. These people will kill you." Jamie and Teven stared at each other and snickered.

Anger rose in Lex's body. He tried to control his alter ego but knew he was going to let go in a matter of seconds due to their obnoxious behavior.

*Hate meeting these friends. Need some new one*s. "What's so funny?" He paused and waited for them to answer.

"Dude, they can't kill minors, it's in the handbook. Didn't you pay attention to anything Mr. Mayfield told us before he left?"

"Yeah man. No older member of the Truson team can attack minors. They can die for that," Jamie said. Teven nodded. Lex tried to replay the comment in his head but couldn't. Technically, he was only here for a couple days after Ford took over as Mandy's personal bodyguard. It was no big deal to him. Right now, there was only one goal in his mind—a cellphone.

"Whatever dude," he said, caring less about the situation. "Please tell me one of you guys have a cell I could use? I need to call my dad."

"Awww, what's the matter? Is someone late for curfew?" Teven teased. Another burst of laughter. Lex wanted to show off his power and kick both of them into another galaxy but decided against it. He sighed. The truth was, he missed some of his old friends back home.

"Just answer the question goofballs."

"Sure, I have one," Teven said. He got out his cell and tossed it to Lex. Lex grabbed it and pushed the numbers on the phone.

"Is your dad all right?" Lex stared at Teven. He thought he might have been joking at first but saw he was concerned by the expression on his face.

"Yeah, I'm pretty sure he's fine. I just need to ask him something, that's all." After four rings, his dad finally picked up.

"Hello?"

"Hi, Dad. It's me, Lex."

"Where the hell have you been? Did you not get my messages?"

"Dad, I'm sorry, okay? Somebody took my phone, and I tried to reach you…"

"Enough with the excuses! I know who confiscated your phone. Ford Mayfield answered when I tried to call you. Care to explain why Ford is still alive? And why does he have your cellphone?" Lex walked to a place a little quieter so his friends wouldn't be able to listen to the conversation.

"Dad, I had every intention of killing him, but one of the members grabbed my phone before I could call you—"

"So, Ford Mayfield grabbed your phone?"

"No. Stin Vanderson did," Lex said. So frustrating. For once in his life why couldn't his dad see he was trying to make him happy?

"Who?"

"Stin Vanderson, he's another member of the Truson team. He was the one who took my phone from me." He paused. "Anyway, that's not the reason I called you."

"Really? I would love to know why you did considering Ford is still alive. Why haven't you found time to kill him?"

"Because I recently found out Mandy is alive," Lex said. There was a long pause at the other end of the phone.

"Dad, are you there?"

"What did you just say?" his father asked.

"I said Mandy's alive. I saw her. She's not dead, she's alive."

"Where is she?"

"She's on the island of Truson. She's alive and Ford's taking care of her. Dad, she's okay," Lex said. Lex focused on his friends strutting toward him.

"Listen to me, Lex. Cancel the plan to kill Ford. I have to find another way, okay?"

"Ooo—kay Dad, so when can I—" Dial tone. Lex stared at the phone before he hung up.

"—Come home?" he finished. Thoughts swirled in his mind about his dad being so short with him. Why was he canceling the plan? What would he come up with next? Whatever plan he was setting up, Lex knew he wasn't going to be able to go home until his next job was done.

That infuriated him.

"Hey Lex, come take a swim with us!"

Lex decided to put his thoughts out of his mind and follow his friends. He needed to take a final break from all of this before he was brought back to reality. Relief flooded through him that he didn't have to kill Ford. Who knew? Maybe his father would come up with another plan—one that involved him staying rich and not having anyone dead in the process.

Sounds like a good plan to me. He ran over to his friends and dived headfirst into the ocean.

***

Mandy stared into Ford's ocean blue eyes. Her chest ached with desire—the kind of passion she always wanted...

"I'm sorry Mandy. I shouldn't have kept secrets from you," he spoke.

"Then why did you?" She felt his hand land on her cheek. She tasted the rich smell of shaving cream and body wash. She stepped back and realized he was dripping wet—tiny droplets cascaded down his skin like rain. Before she could let out a breath, Ford inched closer to her again, this time burying her face in his hands.

"Why do you care so much, Ford?"

"Because you need protection, and I would do anything to protect you," he said. Mandy could feel his hot breath on her face as he inched closer. He lowered his head and gently planted his lips on hers. She immediately felt the electricity surge throughout his body.

The feeling was so intense—her heart raced, her legs tingled, her entire body melted with the deep passion she felt for him—she thought she was going to pass out. Their tongues meshed to the music in their bodies…every stroke she felt sent her higher and higher. While she wanted to live in this beautiful moment, she couldn't help but feel like someone or something was watching her…

"Stay away from him! You will put him in danger!" A voice echoed. "Mandy stop."

"What?" Ford reached for her arm. Mandy backed away. "Mandy, what is it?" Ford turned and saw Tonia smiling. Why?

"Didn't I tell you to leave him alone?" Tonia yelled. Tonia turned to Ford, grabbing him by the neck. She made eye contact with Mandy.

"Now he must die!" Tonia kissed him on the mouth. Bits of green fluid spilled out from his nose and mouth…

Mandy shook her head and studied the window. Huge snowflakes rained outside. She heard a loud boom followed by a few bolts of lightning before she swung her legs over and grunted. She wiped her eyes and face. Memories of the lab invaded her mind. She knew she had been in the lab recovering from the wounds Tonia had inflicted on her. Now she was…where?

"You're back at my place again," Ford said. Ford extended his hand. "Hot cocoa?"

After a couple of sips, she put the mug down on the table.

"I know you're getting tired of being shipped back and forth like this. It's like you're in hibernation or something."

The dream invaded her mind. Bits and pieces of what she remembered made her realize her feelings about Ford. She grappled with what she wanted to say but made a decision that if she wanted to know the answer, the best way to do it was to ask him.

"Do you know who my husband is?"

Ford stopped walking. He cleared his throat and turned his head.

"I'm sorry, what was the question again?"

Yeah right. You're avoiding.

"I think you heard my question, Ford." His eyes lifted to hers. Her legs tingled. *Don't give in. He lied to you, remember? He's keeping secrets. He's not a man you can trust.*

"Who told you?" Ford asked.

"I heard you and Tonia arguing about it. I remember the fight." Mandy shook her head. "I didn't want to believe it at first, but then Tonia confirmed it." Ford cursed and punched the wall. The impact caused the wall to burn, smoke shot straight up when Ford yanked his hand away. Mandy saw traces of blood on his knuckles.

"Are you all right?" Mandy examined the wound.

"I'm fine," he said.

Mandy snapped out of her concern and reevaluated the situation.

"You never answered my question." She watched Ford as he turned to face her.

"It's true. You're married."

Mandy exhaled. She tried to remember something—anything—that confirmed Ford's answer. She got nothing. Married? How could she possibly be married?

Blood surged through her head. She needed answers.

"And when were you going to tell me this?" Ford paused.

"Once you're training was over. We were working so hard the other day, and I didn't want to spoil it—"

"So, you decided to keep it a secret huh? What else have you two been keeping from me?"

Ford's expression changed.

"You don't want to know Mandy, trust me." Mandy walked past him only to give him the perfect opportunity to grab her arm.

"Don't—don't walk away from me like this. Let's talk about it."

Mandy yanked her arm from his grasp.

"Fine. You want to talk about it?" She strolled back to the couch and flopped down. "Let's talk about it. I want to know everything. I want to know what you two have been keeping from me since I got here. How long have you known I was married?" Ford stared at the floor.

"Hello?"

"I didn't know about you being married until I saw an imprint on your finger," he finally answered. "When you mentioned Lex was your son, it sealed what I thought when you woke up from the coma."

"The fact that I'm married?" Pieces of a conversation she had with Tonia were etched in her mind. "Do you know who I'm married to?"

"Yes," he said. "You are married to a man name Vernon Stevenson. He's part of a group called the Transforments." The Transforments. She'd hoped something would pop up like her very short memory of Lex and her, but nothing did. Since he was the first person she recognized, she had quickly come to the conclusion it had to be a memory. She slammed her hands on the couch. Nothing came to her.

"Still don't remember?"

Tears flooded her eyes.

"Shut up!" she screamed. She hid her face. She fought the tears falling from her eyes and sniffed. She fixed her gaze on Ford who was already sitting next to her.

"I'm sorry. I wish I could make it better for you." Mandy pushed strands of her hair aside and placed her hand on her thighs. Just sitting near him made her body feel like she was on fire. What was it about this man that made her feel like she was in high school all over again?

You're angry at him, remember? But when she felt his hand touch her chin and lift it toward him, all the anger she felt melted. His expression showed concern—his eyes were so intense, it felt like he was concentrating on her and nothing else.

"You can. You need to tell me everything you know."

Ford nodded.

"I will tell you everything you need to know under one condition." Mandy got up from the couch.

"No. No more conditions. I want to know everything. You and Dr. Madison have been keeping secrets from me long enough."

"I agree." Silence filled the room between them. "I think you should know everything." He moved toward her until he was standing a few inches away.

"Vernon, your—" he cut the sentence short. His eyes flashed a hint of fiery orange before they shifted back to his natural color. "—husband is the reason why you were discovered in the first place. Dr. Madison found a connection between your husband and my wife's death."

Mandy folded her arms. "How?"

"About ten years ago, there was a Jet Ski accident a couple of miles off the shores of Hawaii. I was there with my—" He stopped.

Mandy stood and waited for him to finish. What was taking so long? "Who were you with in Hawaii?"

"It's hard for me to say this because it still affects me to this day. It's been ten years since it happened, but it still feels like yesterday." Ford's eyes skirted to the activity going on outside. Mandy could tell the snow was getting higher and prayed they wouldn't get snowed in. "Ten years ago, my wife and I went on vacation in Hawaii. We were having problems. She complained about me not spending enough time with her.

"Before the accident, Vernon and I used to be the best of friends. We both worked in the real estate business. I was the new kid on the block. I learned a lot from him."

Mandy saw the orange glow radiating his skin.

"But then he did something to destroy our friendship and quite possibly my relationship with my wife."

What could that possibly be? Mandy wanted to tear her eyes away from the sadness invading Ford's eyes but she couldn't. Ten years of pain etched his face. She reached out and touched him, the contact sending a huge mix of chills and electricity down her spine.

The contact made Ford groan before he took her hand and gently kissed it. Her hands grew weak from the gesture. They were only inches apart, the heat radiating from both of their bodies. The smell of his cologne caused her legs to quiver. She swallowed while he leaned in closer…closer…she felt his hot breath invade her skin. She lifted her chin, so he was able to gain access to her.

So close…all she wanted to do was taste him, to wrap her arms around him…

Please! Please! Please!

Mandy felt his lips press against hers. The kiss was soft, a sign Ford was unsure about the contact. But the minute he opened his mouth, a wave of passion flew through her. She ran her fingers through his hair as she welcomed the invitation. Elements of lust and desire cascaded through both of them. Ford walked forward, causing Mandy to step back toward the couch. Mandy felt Ford's weight on top of her…

The phone rang. Ford got up from Mandy and answered. A part of her didn't want Ford to stop. *You're married.* She repeated the name in her head. *Vernon Stevenson.* The name sounded somewhat familiar to her, but no image popped up in her brain. She remembered Ford telling her she'd suffered from some accident and that she lost her memory. How long was it going to take for her memory to return?

"What do you mean? What are you talking about?" Ford's voice distracted her from her thoughts. "No, that's not true Stin. She's out of town, there's no way she could be dead." Dead? Thoughts swirled while she listened to the conversation. Ford's brows frowned.

"Yes, I do need to see for myself because I don't think she's dead Stin. I also don't believe you're standing over her body."

"Is everything okay?" Mandy asked. She quickly regretted asking when Ford raised his hand up, cutting her off.

"Where are you? I'm coming over right now…so you guys are in Fairbanks?…Stay there, I'll be right over." Ford clicked off his cell.

"What's going on? Who's dead?"

"We need to go…now." Ford grabbed Mandy's arm and tried to escort her to the door.

Mandy pulled out of his grasp. "First of all, you're hurting me. Secondly, I want to know what's going on? Where are we going?"

Ford gritted his teeth. "I don't have time for this." He exhaled. "We have to go now. I will tell you everything once we get there."

Again with the secrets? Why did he have to be so secretive when it came to her? She didn't like it. The look he gave her, however, was enough to make her stop questioning his motives and follow along. She didn't want to piss the guy off more than she already had. As she and Ford headed outside in the snow, Mandy couldn't help but wonder who the person they were going to see was.

***

Dead? Dr. Madison couldn't possibly be dead. Memories of how much they fought clouded his head. He knew he should have explained what was going on to Mandy but right now he was dealing with too many emotions. First, he was forced to conjure up memories of what happened to him and his wife. Now, he had to deal with the possibility of losing one of the best pharmacologists he'd ever known.

The words death and Dr. Madison echoed in his brain.

It couldn't be. This shouldn't be happening right now. Dr. Madison had to be alive. And if she wasn't, there was going to be hell to pay for whoever was involved.

CHAPTER ELEVEN

Ford trekked through the snow on his way to the boat with Mandy speeding behind him. A roar of thunder boomed through the clouds, and the storm got more profound with every step. Ford grunted. The weather outside was precisely how he felt on the inside. Ford thought about his life since he came to Truson S.E.T. He remembered the connection he had with Dr. Madison since he turned into an Orman.

His chest grew tight.

She couldn't be dead. She couldn't be.

"Boy, this snow is picking up speed. How much farther do we have to go before we get to wherever we are going?" Mandy asked.

He needed to go see her to make sure she was really dead.

"Only a few more miles." What kind of answer was that? In reality, he didn't know what time he was going to make it there if he even managed to get to the boat rack at all. Ford started to rethink his decision once he managed to reach the first boat he saw. He stared out into the ocean. Everything was black. The snow made everything worse.

"Uh Ford, I don't think we should go anywhere tonight. The weather's too bad, and we're in the dark. The moonlight is the only thing lighting up everything. Even that's starting to fade away. Can't you wait until it's a little better tomorrow?"

Ford looked out to the horizon. He saw the lights blaring at him. He inched closer and squinted. Apparently, he wasn't the only one traveling in the middle of a massive snowstorm.

"I wonder who else could be traveling in weather like this?" Mandy asked.

"Good question." The boat got closer. He saw Stin's light red hair come into view along with two other members of the team—Su-Lee and Gabriel. As Stin and Gabriel tried to pull out something from the boat, Ford and Mandy rushed to their aid.

Ford's heart sank when he saw the dark brown coffin being lifted from the boat and put into the snow. He still wanted to believe she was alive and all of this was a facade, but when Stin opened the coffin, his worst fears came to light. There she was, her body electrocuted. There were holes throughout her. Whoever it was, he or she did an excellent job of destroying her.

Anger bubbled inside him. He couldn't take his eyes off of her.

"Is that Dr. Madison?" Mandy asked, stepping closer. No one responded to her, so she moved closer. "What happened to her?" she cried.

Ford wanted to soothe the high-pitched voice that escaped her lips. Guilt rippled through him when he thought about what he'd said and done to Dr. Madison before she died. She'd wanted to protect Mandy too.

"She was killed by one of our known enemies. Unfortunately, the enemies we have been hunting are connected to both of you," Stin said.

Ford's eyes shot to Stin.

"Samuel Holifield," Ford said. Fire pounded in his body. His alter ego tore at his skin, wanting so desperately to come out and rip Samuel's body to pieces. Ford turned to Mandy.

"Do you remember anything about him?" Ford got a glimpse of those piercing green eyes and thought about the kiss they shared. He wanted…more. He didn't want to think about the events of today. He tried to forget about Samuel's betrayal of the Truson S.E.T a year after his wife passed away and Samuel became leader of the team. Ford wanted to forget how much Vernon betrayed him on the night of his second honeymoon with his wife.

He wanted to forget the conversation he had the other night with Vernon when it came to his son Lex and all the threats he made…

"The name sounds familiar," Mandy said. "But as far as remembering what he looks like, nothing." Silence filled the air before Stin gently patted Ford on the back.

"I know this is hard for you, just as it is for the rest of us, but I need to know if you talked to Vernon at all?"

"Yes," he replied.

"What did you guys say to each other?"

Snippets of the conversation echoed in his head.

"Vernon told me he wanted his son back and if I didn't do as he asked, he was going to send me a warning."

"You threatened him?" Ford could hear the answer looming in his mind.

"No, I didn't. Vernon was under the impression I had hurt Lex—"

"—Because of his cell," Stin finished. "So in his mind, he thought you had harmed Lex in some way."

"Yes. I tried to reassure him I didn't, but Vernon must have thought otherwise. I did threaten him by telling him when I found him, I was going to rip his head off."

Stin touched the bridge of his nose. "I'm sure that didn't go well."

Su-Lee stared at both of them. "Obviously not. I could be wrong, but I think you pissing him off on him is the reason why Dr. Madison—"

"—Is dead. Dr. Madison is dead, and it's all my fault. Don't hesitate to speak your mind, Su-Lee."

"That's not what I was going to say. I just made the connection, I'm not saying it's your fault at all." Su-Lee's high-pitched voice told Ford she was afraid of him, a reaction he was disturbed by. Ford shifted his weight and stared at his feet until he felt a hand touch his shoulder.

"Ford, look at me, buddy." Ford came face-to-face with Stin but discovered it wasn't Stin's hand on his shoulder. "I don't blame you for what happened. None of us do. We didn't think Vernon would be such a coward as to run back to Samuel and tell him what happened."

"We can read each other's minds, but we can't read the minds of our enemies." Ford heard Tonia groan, and all eyes focused on her.

"Tonia." Stin paused. "I'm surprised it's taken you this long to find us."

"Shut up Stin," she snapped and inched closer to Ford but stopped herself when she saw the coffin. "Who's—who's in there?"

The air stood still.

"It's Dr. Madison," Ford said. Tonia's eyes grow more prominent. Tears flowed down her cheeks.

Have to get out of here. Have to distract myself from this. Ford was surprised when he felt Mandy's hand glide to his back.

Such small comfort from a horrific situation.

The next few minutes were the worst he'd witnessed since becoming an Orman. As Tonia ran to the coffin in tears, all Ford wanted to do was tear himself apart. His alter ego grew stronger.

So did his power.

Have to get out of here…

"I have to go." Ford broke contact with Mandy and darted toward the ocean. He could hear Mandy's voice trail behind him, followed by Stin, Su-Lee and eventually Tonia telling him to come back. Ford quickened his pace and transformed into an orca moments before his body landed in the water…

***

She wasn't supposed to feel anything for him. He had betrayed her by keeping secrets from her…secrets that revealed a lot about her past. This would have been the perfect opportunity to find an escape route and go back to where she came from. But despite Ford almost confessing what happened to his dead wife, she still couldn't remember her so-called husband. The only thing she could remember was the horrible nightmares she suffered within the last three days.

The only relief she got was from her memory she had of her and Ford last night kissing.

And they say dreams could never come true…

She needed to stay away from him—not because of what he did to her (although she was still pissed about that one) but because of what Tonia told her. If what Tonia said was the truth, Ford's life, as well as the other members of the Truson S.E.T., were in grave danger. The guilt Ford felt about Dr. Madison being gone from this earth didn't compare to the hurt she felt on the inside.

Comfort him. He needs you.

"You did this!" Mandy turned. She didn't get a chance to speak her mind before Tonia pushed her into the snow. Tonia wrapped her hands around Mandy's neck.

"You did this! I told you to stay away from us…I told you to stay away from him, but you just wouldn't listen. Now Dr. Madison is dead!" Air flew out of Mandy's lungs. She touched both of Tonia's wrists. Electricity shot through Tonia's arms. It traveled throughout her entire body. Tonia screamed until Stin threw a huge snowball, causing her to collapse on the ground next to Dr. Madison.

"Tonia!" Su-Lee ran toward her and held her. "Stin, you have to be careful with her, she's fragile."

"Fragile my ass, that's the second time she's attacked Mandy. She needs to control herself. We don't have time for this. Samuel knows we're onto him and so does Vernon. It's not going to take them long to find out about Mandy if they haven't done so already."

"So, what do we do?" Su-Lee asked.

"We have no other choice but to fight. We need to be prepared. A war is coming, and there's no way Vernon's gonna listen to reason. Neither are we." Stin turned. "But first we have to find him."

Mandy prayed Stin wouldn't ask her to find Ford alone. She was a bundle of emotions right now and going after Ford didn't seem like a good idea. *But he could be in danger. You have to find him.* Blood rushed through her body. The possibilities of him out there alone and vulnerable turned her stomach.

What if Samuel or Vernon killed him? Mandy imagined the vision playing out in her mind and shivered. She couldn't live with that. She'd only known him for a couple of days, and already she was starting to have feelings for him.

She had to find him.

"Let's go. Everyone change into orcas and find Ford. He's gonna need us. He cannot be alone. We have to find him." Mandy and Tonia were the first to run to the water. *This woman is pathetic.* The way she followed Ford everywhere she went, the goofy smiles she gave out whenever Ford looked her way…

And yet Ford wasn't into her. How sad. She needed to get over it and move on.

Mandy felt her alter ego rip through her clothes and throughout her body while she dived headfirst into the water. She heard a splash, giving an indication Tonia was not too far behind.

I'll find him first and maybe, just maybe, it will be enough to finally keep him away from you.

You do know he's not that into you, right? Apparently, you have some indication of that, considering he's always around me.

Guys, this is no time to be switching thoughts about who Ford wants more. Right now, we have to find him before Samuel and the Transforments rip him apart," Stin interrupted.

Mandy tried to turn off the voices in her head so she could concentrate on finding Ford, but it wasn't working. She sensed the team behind her and remembered what Ford said about whales traveling in pods so whenever danger lurked, they would be ready to fight whoever came their way.

It was a good strategy.

After letting the deep waters of the Arctic Ocean massage her body, Mandy felt a stab of pain under her belly. The pain was followed by a burning sensation she thought was never going to end. Something wasn't right. The excitement she felt stirred the electricity inside her.

A rush of emotions flooded through her. *He's in trouble. Got to…get to…him now!* Mandy pumped her flippers as hard as she could, her body soaring through the water. She searched through another pod of orcas to see if she could locate Ford.

Nothing. Pressure started building in her chest.

Have to find him. He's in danger. Have to find him. Not if I find him first.

Images of him being attacked by another group of orcas flashed like a movie scene. There had to be at least ten orcas battling Ford. She saw them opening their mouths and powers to rip Ford apart. Mandy searched for him again. Her heart pounded against her chest when she spotted an orca swimming alone.

Ford.

She knew the difference between him and the other orcas. During the training, Ford mentioned the glow on their bellies, each glow representing the power each member had. Her power was blue for electricity. Ford's was orange for fire. Ford briefly mentioned Stin and Tonia but just gathering enough information from their patterns, she realized Tonia's glow was green matching the color of her poison.

Stin, she wasn't so sure about.

Mandy focused on Ford. Danger lurked as the pods started forming around him. Mandy checked to see if there were any signs of color on their bellies. She couldn't tell either way.

"It's them."

"Who?"

"The Transforments. They're here," Tonia said, invading everyone's thoughts.

"Where? I don't see them." Stin's voice radiated through her brain. Mandy stayed on the pod, moving in closer to Ford who apparently seemed oblivious to the whole situation. Couldn't he sense the danger he was in? Well if he couldn't, she could. There was no way she could ever let them hurt him.

"What do you see Mandy?"

"A pod of orcas. They're surrounding Ford. Planning a sneak attack. We have to hurry before it's too late."

"Agreed," Stin replied. Mandy was only a couple of feet away from him when she saw one of the orcas attack Ford, its mouth biting hard and fast into the middle of Ford's body.

"Ford!"

As one orca attacked him from the side, another one attacked him from behind. Electricity started flowing throughout his body. Mandy felt a massive jolt inside of herself. She was feeling what Ford was going through.

Must stop it.

Mandy was the first one to strike. She held her grip on the orca who was the first to have a hold on Ford. She opened her mouth and held tight, hoping her electricity would be stronger than theirs so they would back off.

Mandy, get back!

She could hear Ford's panicked thoughts, and heat radiated through her face. Within the last few seconds, a huge fireball formed around Ford's body. A burning sensation fueled her body until she broke contact seconds before the huge fireball spread out and burned three of the orcas who made contact with him. Mandy swam back as far as she could, the fireball within inches of reaching her. She sensed the rest of the Truson S.E.T. fighting back against the other orcas who came near Ford.

She gathered her strength and charged again, not sure whether the orca was an enemy or not. She needed to make sure Ford was safe. *Concentrate. Remember what the goal is*. Voices raged in her head as the rest of the team gave commands to each other at a moment's notice.

The orca's heart stopped beating. Mandy let go and watched the body sink to the bottom of the ocean floor. She couldn't describe the feelings bubbling inside her while she continued attacking the other orcas crossing their path.

"How many are there?" Stin asked.

"It looks to be ten or twenty."

"Ten or twenty, Tonia? Can you please be accurate? I need to know how many to fight off!"

"Well, I can't see with all this smoke," Tonia replied.

"Mandy, how are you doing over there? Are you okay?" Stin asked.

Dust and ash finally evaporated into the water making everything more explicit for her to attack again. Ford swam back from one orca and slammed into another. Mandy watched as another orca, this one all white, dug his teeth into Stin until his entire body became frozen. Mandy jerked herself back into focus when she felt an orca bump into her.

That's why you're no good for Ford. Always so distracted by everything coming your way. Don't you ever pay attention to anything? Tonia scoffed.

Anger rose in Mandy's chest while Tonia battled yet another orca, clearly showing her and everyone else her power. Despite the help she was giving Ford, Ford managed to do everything on his own. Mandy decided the best thing to do was to ignore Tonia and the lingering thoughts looming in her head about Ford not needing her and keep fighting. She was getting ready to attack more orcas who seemed to be a threat to her when a voice invaded her thoughts.

"If you continue to live this life, I would suggest you tell your friends to back off Mandy," A voice crept in.

"You leave her alone. If you want a fight, you need to deal with me. Come out and show your true self so we can end this," Ford said.

Very well.

Mandy watched the orca spring out of the water and do a flip in mid-air before finally landing on the snow. Ford swam to the edge of the shore before he leaped into the air and transformed back into his alter ego. The rest of the team followed. Mandy decided to give it a try by swimming to the edge of the shore. She felt the water draining out of her system. She couldn't breathe.

"Think about transforming before you do it," Su-Lee said. Mandy thought about being human again and sure enough, her body stretched back to her human form.

"Thanks."

"No problem." Su-Lee extended her hand. "I'm Su-Lee."

Mandy shook her hand. "Mandy."

"Well, since we're all getting acquainted, I believe Mandy knows who I am—right Mandy?" Mandy gawked at the man with the gray eyes and light silvery white hair that flowed over his neck.

"She doesn't remember you. Maybe that's for a good reason," Ford interjected.

A slight grin formed on Samuel's face.

"Really? Now that's interesting. You mean to tell me she's been here all this time and doesn't remember anything?" Samuel tilted his head to the side. Mandy never took her eyes off of him. The gray eyes, the white hair…she was starting to remember the frequent conversations Samuel had with Vernon, conversations she wasn't a part of.

She never knew why everything was so secretive until now. Samuel and Vernon were Ormans too, but on different sides of the law—whatever that law was. Mandy tried to figure out why they kept the secret for so long. Did they think about how she would have reacted? Or was it because they were trying to protect her from something else?

"Yes, I do," Mandy said. "You were my husband's boss. You were the leader of some sort—the Trans—"

"Transforments," Samuel corrected. Samuel made eye contact with Ford. "Seems like she knows more than you think."

"And I'm more than sure that the sight of you is making her sick to her stomach."

"Oh, is that how you feel, Ford?" He shrugged his shoulders. "Well, I can't say I'm surprised considering how much you betrayed me by kicking me out of the group."

"You murdered innocent members of the Truson Super Elite Team to become the leader!" Stin exclaimed.

Samuel laughed at his suggestion.

"Is it true Samuel?" Mandy watched Samuel stop laughing and gawk at her.

"Who cares if it's true or not? Frankly, I don't care what they think."

"Answer the question!" Mandy yelled. She needed to know what else they had been hiding for the last few days.

"All right. It shouldn't matter since you won't last very long anyway." Samuel exhaled. "It's true. I murdered several members back in—" Samuel put a finger up to his chin and looked up at the sky. "—I don't exactly remember the date but I think it was three years ago." Samuel's face changed. "Boy did I love those years. Killing all of those people was fun for me, which probably wouldn't have even happened if they had voted to make me the leader of the team."

"It wasn't going to happen Samuel. You never followed our orders. You always did what you wanted without consideration of other people," Su-Lee said.

"Those people deserved what they got. They kept testing me and my powers. Obviously, I had to show them who was boss."

"Can we just kill him already?" Tonia asked. She flipped her light brown hair to her back. "I'm already bored with this story."

Ford ignored her.

"I know what you did in the past, and I know what you're trying to do now. It won't work. I won't let Mandy get killed for whatever scheme you're cooking up." The wind shifted the snow in the air, causing Mandy's face to sting. Ford took one final look at her before he faced Samuel again. "It's over Samuel. You need to accept it and leave us alone."

Tension filled the air.

Samuel scoffed.

"I'm afraid I can't do that. You and your fellow minions have officially destroyed me and my fellow clan, the Transforments. I think that deserves some type of punishment, don't you?" Before Ford could answer, Samuel continued. "Then you interrupted me when I was telling Mandy my glorious days of being a member of the team. How rude can you be, Ford?"

Mandy felt her power getting stronger by the minute. Memories of him flashed through her mind. Tonia was right. She'd heard enough, and she wanted a piece of him.

"Well, no worries. I guess you will never hear the end of my story since it's time for one of our groups to die and I have a pretty good feeling it won't be mine."

Mandy watched the members of the Transforments come out of the water one-by-one, the snow not phasing them one bit. They took careful steps and positioned themselves directly behind Samuel. It felt like hours before all of them stood behind him, ready to fight in an instant. Her alter ego ripped inside her, ready to come out again.

A sly grin formed on Samuel's face.

"Let's begin."

CHAPTER TWELVE

The Transforments didn't hold back.

Electricity sprung from the air, creating substantial electrical currents that lit up the night sky. Ford's alter ego heightened every sense he had. The Transforments came at full speed two to three at a time. He created a fireball and threw it in the crowd. It made contact with two of the members, sending them into a halo of fire and ash. It didn't take long for them to die from the impact. Though a third one was hit, he still managed to swipe a strong current of electricity through Ford's chest.

"That's it Leron. Show him how it's truly done," Samuel said, his voice flooding through Ford's eardrums. The contact stopped when a large current struck Leron, sending him crashing into the ocean. Once Ford was able to catch his breath, he searched through the massive crowd. His chest caught in his throat when he saw Mandy standing in the middle of all the chaos, her head tilted back and her arms extended out to her sides.

What the hell is she doing? Is she trying to get herself killed? Ford's mind raced at the possibility of someone—anyone—trying to kill her. His stomach flipped. Blood pummeled his insides. *Can't let her die.*

Ford lurched at Mandy, his body leaping through the air, arms outstretched hoping he could reach her in time…

Too late.

The moment Ford made contact with Mandy, a massive tunnel of lightning exploded from her chest, causing Ford to fly back into the air along with a few members of the Transforments. Ford saw half of them land on top of the snow, the other half flying into the ocean. Ford needed to stop her before the members of the Truson S.E.T. got hurt. That moment flew out the window when his head crashed into the snow. Ford tried to keep his eyes open as much as possible but couldn't. His vision was blurry. Everything started spinning in his mind.

"Mandy stop!" a voice shouted. Ford didn't recognize whose voice it was. Stin? Su-Lee? Tonia? The voice repeated itself.

"Mandy stop!"

"I know how to make her stop."

"No Tonia. You've done enough. If you hurt her again, I'll kill you myself," Stin said.

"Then what do you want us to do Stin? If we don't stop her, she's going to kill us all."

"No, she won't! I'll stop her," Stin said. Ford closed his eyes. He could hear voices clearly now but still couldn't see.

Can't let them hurt her. Have to protect her.

He needed to communicate with her somehow. Maybe he could still connect with her mentally like he did before. Ford took a couple of deep breaths. He thought about wrapping his arms around her and gently whispering in her ear to stop. The thought of her being so close to him rattled him in ways he couldn't imagine.

Mandy, you have to stop. Ford could feel himself slipping away from her. The darkness had settled in. They were so far away…

Ford closed his eyes.

***

Mandy couldn't stop the powers escaping from her body. The experience was both scary and excruciating. She couldn't remember when she had so much control over anything. She tried her best to pull back her powers so no one else would get hurt.

Except for the Transforments.

But try as she might, her powers were taking on a life of their own. Mandy hadn't seen a reason why she needed the training with Ford after she got here. She thought the whole thing was senseless. Undoubtedly, she was able to control herself without any help.

After tonight, however, she knew that was not the case.

She kept hearing Stin and Tonia's voices in the background but no Ford. Where was he? Shouldn't he be the one stopping her instead of Stin, or worse, Tonia? She tried to pull back her power to concentrate on what was happening with Ford but couldn't. To her, it felt like she was having an out of body experience. Her mind was entirely into it, but her body was somewhere else. Mandy tried again.

Nothing.

Ford, where are you? Help me, please. If she wanted anyone to rescue her, it would be him. He was the only person she trusted to stop her from losing herself. Her panic went into full gear when she suddenly felt a massive shift of wind and ice surrounding her. Her powers were getting weaker.

So was she.

Then like a flick of a switch, the cold air froze. The ground shook violently. Mandy's powers stopped, and she gaped at the enormous white boulder rolling toward her. Her body wouldn't budge. The boulder crashed into her legs. The horrible impact sent her flying face first into the snow. The mix of water and burnt flesh invaded her nostrils. She coughed. A set of footsteps crashed into the snow as the members raced to her rescue.

"Mandy, are you all right? Please tell me you're okay." Mandy's head shot up. She turned. Relief flooded through her when she stared into Lex's gray eyes. She lifted herself off of the snow.

"Mandy?" Lex was waiting for her answer. With one arm around his waist, Mandy pulled Lex into a hug.

"Thank you for saving me," she whispered. The embrace was short-lived because she spotted Ford's body on the ground, blood spewing from his skull. His eyes were open, but he wasn't moving.

What have I done?

Mandy kneeled at Ford's side and stroked his hair. She lifted his head up and uncovered the massive mass of blood on her hands.

"I told you, you were dangerous for him! You wouldn't listen to me! First, it was Samuel who only came out here because of your violent ex-husband Vernon, now this. You killed him!" Tonia screamed. Mandy rose to her feet.

"Will you just shut up? How stupid can you be, huh?" Mandy inched closer to her.

"Do you not realize that he's not into you? How does it feel to know you love someone with all your heart, but he doesn't love you in return?"

Tears streamed down Tonia's face. Mandy couldn't help but feel sorry for her. A part of her felt bad for the outburst, but this wasn't the time to argue with her about it. She needed to help Ford.

"Enough, both of you. We need to focus on Ford right now. He's in bad shape. The best thing you two can do is try to save his life—together," Su-Lee said.

"I agree." Mandy shifted her weight and got back into the same position as before. "He needs help. If he doesn't get it soon, he's going to die because—" Mandy swallowed. "Because of what I've done." Lex shook his head.

"Mandy, this isn't your fault. You didn't do this on purpose." Lex put his hand on Mandy's shoulder. "I know the guilt is eating you alive, but we need to save Ford."

"He's right." Tonia sniffed. "We have to work together on this." '

Stin walked past them and lifted Ford up from the snow only to reveal an enormous rock poking out of the snow. Stin grabbed one arm and leaned it over his shoulder. Mandy raced over and grabbed his other arm. She held onto Ford with all the strength she could muster and pushed herself through the dense snow.

Soon Tonia, Lex, and the others followed behind them, offering to help. Because his feet were dragging, Lex and Tonia decided to lift higher. During the trip, Mandy noticed Samuel's burnt lifeless body lying in a puddle of water.

She shuddered. They were all silent until they finally made the trip to the Truson Headquarters. Everyone helped lift him onto the bed.

"We have to stop the blood," Tonia said. "If we don't do it fast, he'll die."

"I know how to handle that." Stin lifted the back of Ford's head with his hands. "I can freeze the blood to make sure he doesn't bleed out completely. Mandy!" Mandy's eyes lifted from Ford to Stin.

"I need you to go into the cabinets downstairs and get me forty milligrams of Binosil now. Do you understand?" Mandy shook her head.

"No, I can't leave him like this. I can't—"

"I'll go with her," Tonia said. "Mandy, if you want to save his life, I would suggest you come with me now." Mandy thought about the offensive threats from Tonia. She was right. She needed to stay away from him. She was the whole reason he was lying in a hospital bed with no sign of life. She couldn't tell if he was breathing this very moment.

"Mandy, I need you to listen to me. Ford needs the Binosil *now*. If he doesn't get it within the next few minutes, he will die and won't come back." Before Mandy could argue, Tonia's arm pulled her out the door and down the flight of stairs.

"I don't know why Ford seems to be so fascinated with you considering how you reacted in there, but I guess that's none of my business, is it?"

Mandy didn't respond. All this time, her life had been consistently in danger...danger that almost led to Ford's death. Her being married to a possible murderer made the whole situation unbearable. Mandy's thoughts shifted when Tonia dragged her to the storage room and flicked on the lights. Visions of freezers storing all kinds of liquids and needles caught her attention.

"What are we looking for again?"

"Binosil. It's a drug Dr. Madison used to heal us whenever we were injured." Tonia punched the numbers into the system. The double doors flew open. Tonia switched places with Mandy, shoving Mandy in front of her.

"Look through the bottles and find forty milligrams of Binosil. Hurry up, Ford's life is on the line," she said. Mandy sprang into action, searching the bottles until she found the blue liquid. She grabbed a couple of needles off the tray and headed for the door.

"Let's go." By the time Tonia was able to catch up to her, she had already made it back into the room. She gave the needle to Stin. Stin took it and was about to inject Ford when a female doctor entered and examined Ford's eyes with a penlight. She started jotting down notes on her clipboard.

"What do we have here?"

"Uh…This man was injured in a battle a few miles away on the island and might have suffered some sort of concussion," Mandy said, wondering where the woman came from. The doctor put on some rubber gloves and lifted Ford's head.

"Hey, you might want to be careful. He's suffering some serious injuries here," Stin said.

Mandy watched Stin focus on her name tag. "Who are you anyway?"

The doctor gently laid his head back on the pillow.

"I'm his doctor, that's who."

More notes.

Mandy felt uneasy about her. For her to just spring out of nowhere was a cause for concern.

"This man is going to need surgery stat." The doctor grabbed onto the bed and started to drag it to the door, but Mandy stopped her by grabbing both of her hands.

"Where do you think you're going with him?"

"I would like to know the answer to that myself," Tonia said.

"You have every right not to trust her. She's a phony." All eyes were on Lex as he ran inside. A strong odor of dead meat and blood filled the air. His clothes were torn from the chest down.

"I don't know what this young man is talking about—"

"Give Ford the Binosil. He should be okay within a couple of hours. Get him out of here," Lex said.

"But what about you? You can't fight her alone—"

"—and he won't!" Two other boys popped up behind him. One was chubby with short, curly light brown hair. The other was a tall, skinny redhead whose hair looked like Carrot Top. "That's what we're here for."

Stin stuck the needle into Ford's arm despite the protest from the doctor. Then he turned to the three boys standing in the doorway. "What are you two doing here? Aren't you guys supposed to be off practicing somewhere?"

The chubby one threw Lex to the side and cleared his throat.

"We're here to save our professor from a lifetime of hell or death." He paused. "In other words, this doctor is working for Vernon."

"Where's Gabriel? We need him to guard Ford. If Vernon knows where Ford and Mandy are, he won't hesitate to kill them both." Tonia stepped in front of them.

"You three need to go and hide someplace safe. We don't want you getting in the way of our plan."

"I can take care of her. I know what to do," Lex said. He leaned in closer so his other two buddies wouldn't be able to hear him.

"Let me handle her please." Tonia hesitated. Mandy felt her stomach flip-flop. She couldn't take it anymore.

She was starting to feel like a burden to everyone, including Ford.

The man that she reluctantly had fallen in love with.

The thought of losing him became too much for her to bear. Lex risking his life for her made her ill. She took a couple of deep breaths to control herself. She gently placed her hand on top of Ford's and felt his body getting warmer. *If he makes it through, I'll walk away. I'll go find my husband and try to work things out to protect Ford.*

The thought didn't make sense to her. She couldn't remember who she was married to. How could she make a promise like that when she didn't even know what her husband looked like?

"Get those three out of here now! I don't want them causing any more trouble tonight. We have too much going on right now, and I don't need any more distractions!" Stin and Mandy waited to see if there were any signs of recovery.

Nothing. She heard Lex and the other two boys arguing about being kicked out but was reassured by Stin that Tonia could take them back to the cabin.

"So, is what the boys are saying true? Are you working for Vernon?"

The doctor put her hands up.

"I have no idea who that is. I've never heard of Vernon. This is the first time I've been here, honest." Su-Lee strolled toward her and took a look at her badge. Stin, Su-Lee, and Mandy shot a look at each other.

"Can you come with me, please?" Su-Lee smiled.

The woman shifted her weight.

"Look, I really don't have time to have a meeting with you right now. This patient needs—"

"Don't worry, Stin and I can figure out what he needs," Mandy said. "I think you should just go with Su-Lee." Fear invaded the woman's eyes while Su-Lee dragged her out the door.

"Wait, I swear I'm not who you think I am. I'm a real doctor." The woman screamed and continued screaming down the hallway. Mandy could only imagine what Su-Lee had done to her. Chills went down her spine.

"Since when did you become the boss?" Stin asked.

Mandy stared at Ford, completely ignoring the question. "Mandy?"

"When is he going to wake up?" Mandy asked. She shook her head. "I don't know what happened to me back there. I completely lost control." Mandy ran her hands through her hair. "It was like I was having an out of body experience. I tried to control it and I couldn't and now—" Mandy stopped herself short. She squeezed Ford's hand. "I just want him to be okay."

Stin placed his hand on her shoulder. "And he will be."

Mandy shifted. Despite the close contact, she didn't take her eyes off of Ford.

"The Binosil will work. He'll come back to us."

And by that time, I'll be gone. A small ache formed in Mandy's chest. She remembered the kiss they shared and how things could have been different between them. If she wasn't married to her husband who was out to kill them both, maybe she could have given them a chance.

But with Vernon catching up to them, and after what happened with Samuel and her powers, she knew she was a constant danger Ford didn't need.

Mandy stood over his body and leaned forward to give him a peck on the forehead.

Goodbye Ford. I will miss you.

"I'm gonna go for a walk."

Stin nodded.

With one piercing look at Ford, she walked out the door and headed back to the cabin.

***

Lex and his two friends landed hard on the snow. Lex knew that the team members were strong but having all three of them being carried out and thrown into the snow at the same time was ridiculous. Mean. Cruel. How dare Stin kick him and his friends out of the room? And to say he didn't want any more trouble out of him after all he'd done to protect Mandy?

The man was downright selfish.

"Was that really necessary? All you had to do was ask us to leave," Teven said. He dusted the snow off of himself and glared at Tonia with such anger, Lex thought of using his powers to fling her into the ocean somewhere.

That sounded like a good idea.

"I'm sorry. I didn't really mean to cause any harm, but I have to do what's best for the team. You three are a liability we just can't afford to have right now," Tonia said.

Lex could tell she was enjoying this. Sweet and vile. "A liability? I just saved my—" Lex paused, unsure if Tonia knew the truth or not. "—Mandy from completely losing herself. If it wasn't for me, all of you would be dead right now."

"The dude's right," Jamie said. "I think you should listen to what he has to say." Tonia opened her mouth to say something but stopped. The most horrible ringtone invaded Lex's ears like a bomb. His friend picked up the phone.

"Hello? Yeah…he used my phone to talk to you the other day, that's probably why you didn't recognize the number…"

"Who is that?" Tonia barked. She grimaced. Lex was starting to understand why Stin didn't like her. She was cold-hearted and didn't care about anyone but herself.

Much like his father.

Teven shoved the phone over to him. "It's your dad."

"Perfect." Tonia snatched the phone and put it up to her ear. "Well, isn't this a lovely surprise Mr. Stevenson. Who would have thought you were smart enough to track us down…no your son is here but unfortunately, he's been held captive by us…If you want your son to come home, I would suggest you show yourself and prove to us you're not a coward…" Lex tried to grab the phone from her, but Tonia put her finger up, warning him to stay back.

"If you don't show yourself within the next few days, then I'll have no other choice but to kill him and bury his body someplace where you will never find him."

Lex grimaced. He didn't like the way the conversation was going. He wanted to settle this himself, he was old enough to do that. Why everyone wanted to treat him like he was a child, he'd never know. One thing he did know was he was growing tired of everyone here.

And the better alternative would be what? Being your father's puppet all day long?

Lex shuddered. Somehow that option sounded way worse than being on an island with people he knew wanted his father dead. Maybe that was a good thing for him considering how awful his father had treated him throughout the years because of his condition.

Don't forget how much he uses you every time he wants something—like to kill Ford to support his lavish lifestyle.

A job he was supposed to do two days ago but never found the time…

"You want to talk to him to confirm my statement?" Tonia gave a sly grin. Lex felt his alter ego pulling at him to come out and rip Tonia's face off.

"Sure, he's right here." Tonia extended her arm to Lex. "Telephone. I think we already know who it is, right?"

Lex snatched the phone.

"Hi, Dad, what's up? Yeah, I'm still here on the island, and…well yeah, I told you she's…" Lex cut the conversation short and turned to Tonia.

Tonia raised a brow. "Please, don't stop on my account. I would love to know what you two are talking about."

"Hey." Teven pointed his finger at Tonia. "This is none of your business. This is between a boy and his father, something you couldn't possibly understand" He swayed his body back and forth and nodded his head. "How do you like those apples?" Teven asked. Tonia smiled and nodded until she grabbed him by the shirt.

"Talk to me like that again and I'll personally make it my business to poison you until you beg for mercy, do you understand?"

His eyes bulged. He nodded.

Lex decided to move away from the situation so no one else could hear the conversation between him and his father.

"I told you she's alive Dad, I saw her…No, I haven't gotten around to killing Ford yet but…Dad c'mon, you have to give me more time…"

"Do you think I'm stupid Lex? I know you've been doing nothing but hanging out with those bastards you like to call your newfound friends. I don't have time for this. I sent you to do a job, and I expect it to be done quickly."

"Dad, you don't have to worry anymore. Samuel's dead," Lex said. There was a long pause at the other end. "Plus, you told me to sit tight and not do anything after I told you about Mandy."

A big mistake on my part.

"How did Samuel die? How could you let this happen?"

"There was no choice in the matter—"

"No choice? And here I thought you would appreciate the things I've done for you over the years, but now I just see you are the same coward as the Truson Super Elite Team.”

“Dad—”

“I just wanted a son who was normal. A son who could run and play with the other children in the daylight without being burned or blinded by the light. I wanted a son who I could be proud of and who had the same skin complexion as mine, not someone I’m ashamed of.”

The blood rushed throughout Lex's body. He balled up his fists. “Dad, don’t do this—”

“Don’t do what? You’re nothing but trash. Your mother should have killed you before you were born you pathetic freak.”

“How dare you talk to me like that?” Lex’s throat burned. Tears formed in his eyes, but he rubbed them before they reached his cheeks.

“You know what? I’ve tried so hard to impress you by doing this job for you even though I knew it was wrong. I tried to please you so you could finally accept me as your son,” Lex said. His voice cracked, but he maintained control by swallowing the lump in the back of his throat.

“Stop crying like a baby, Lex. I was trying to teach you how to be a man.”

“By murdering people? That’s your definition of being a man? If it is, then I don’t want to be your son. I wish I was never born to such an evil bastard like you!” Lex heard Vernon laughing in his ear. He gripped the phone tighter.

"You know what I hope? I hope Ford and the rest of the Truson Super Elite Team find you and destroy you and everything you love!"

"Careful son, that includes you," Vernon said, his voice low and bitter and full of hatred. He laughed again.

"I hope you die cause when you do, I will spit on your grave."

"Enough!" A voice rang out.

Lex focused his attention on the sound and stared straight at Mandy. Mandy inched closer to Lex.

"That's enough Lex. You need to apologize to your father right now. We're going home."

CHAPTER THIRTEEN

"Gone? What do you mean she's gone?"

Stin shifted his feet. Uncertainty was written all over his face. He tried to process what he wanted to say, but Ford wasn't going to let him off the hook so quickly. Stin shrugged.

"One minute I was talking to her about you, reassuring her you were going to be fine then the next minute, she was gone. I couldn't find her anywhere man."

"You searched for her by *yourself?* Where were the others?"

Stin pointed to the door with his thumb. "Well, Tonia decided to stay with you after I stopped her from ripping Lex's friends apart." Ford processed that thought. He reminded himself of having a long talk with her once he found Mandy.

"What about Su-Lee and Gabriel? Where were they?" Ford barked. Where was his team when he needed them the most? His face grew hot. He expected his team to do whatever it took to protect Mandy while he was recovering from his wounds. Now he was standing in a room with his best friend telling him Mandy left without his permission.

Not acceptable.

"Su-Lee stayed and watched over you while Gabriel and I took turns searching the parameters of the island." He paused. "We also had to find Dr. Madison's coffin and bring it back to the Truson Headquarters so we can discuss the funeral arrangements." Ford's heart ached at Stin's comment. He didn't want to deal with Dr. Madison being gone. He had enough when it came to Roxanne.

"Tonia stayed here too. She kept checking on you every hour to see if you woke up." Stin snorted. "I don't know what's going on with that woman, but I think you seriously need to talk to her."

"Tonia is the least of my concerns. I want you to go find Mandy—now!" When Stin didn't move, Ford continued. "I need you to take some of your team members with you—Gabriel and Su-Lee might be a good fit considering I need to have a talk with—" Ford cut himself off. What the hell was he doing? He needed to find her himself. He couldn't trust his own team to keep her guarded and protected against his enemies before, why should he believe them now?

"A talk with who?"

"Never mind, I'll find her myself," Ford said. He limped to the door.

"Dude, if you're going to go out there, at least put on some clothes!" Stin shouted behind him. Ford's eyes went to his wardrobe. Stin had a point. The hospital gown was partially open. He knew he could survive in the snow but only after a specific time.

He needed clothes.

He needed *her*.

"Good luck!"

Ford ignored his friend and ran back to the cabin. He remembered how he felt when he opened his eyes after the dream he had. Ford dreamed of her being inside him, their bodies pressing together like flowers, their lips intertwining to the desire he fought so long to bury. He didn't want to admit it at first because of the betrayal he felt toward Roxanne. He'd promised her he would never love another woman the way he loved her.

Now that promise was broken.

Ford didn't have time to process what that meant. All he knew was he couldn't live with the possibility of losing her. His stomach churned. He cursed. *She has to be okay.* He thought. *If he lay one finger on her, I'll kill him myself.*

Ford knocked down the door with his weight and headed upstairs. He grabbed the first clothes he saw and shoved himself into them. It was only when he searched for a pair of socks that he found the gold wedding band sitting on the dresser staring back at him. He picked it up and examined it, the words reflecting in the sunlight. "To my dearest husband, Ford Michael Mayfield. I will love you forever."

His chest tightened.

I will love you forever too.

It was hard to move on, but Ford knew Roxanne didn't want him to spend the rest of his life alone. She would want him to be happy and to find someone worthy of his love. He gently opened up the drawer and carefully put the ring inside before shutting it closed. His mind focused on finding Mandy as he headed out the door. He thanked the heavens it wasn't snowing outside like the night before. He could quickly take a Jet Ski to go find her.

Where was he to begin?

Apparently, she left without telling anyone, meaning she had snuck off somewhere without a trace. She didn't want to be found. *Too bad. I don't care if I have to search around the world ten times over, I will find you and bring you back home to me Mandy Stevenson.* He made a note to himself about changing her last name once all of this was over and headed toward the row of Jet Skis on the far corner of the island.

"Do you need some help finding her?" Ford paused and circled around to see Tonia dressed in an all-white gown except for her light brown hair swaying from the wind drifting around the island.

Ford shrugged. "I don't know if I need your help right now Tonia. The last thing I want is for you to go another round with Mandy." Ford turned and proceeded toward his destination.

"Ford, I'm sorry. I didn't mean to hurt you!" Tonia cried. "You have to believe I did everything I could to keep her on the island—" Ford galloped his way back to her.

"Don't you dare lie to me, Tonia! Not now, not ever!" he said, pointing his finger in her face. Tonia stepped a few inches back from him and stumbled into the snow. Ford exhaled and buried his face in his hands.

"Why Tonia? Why would you hurt Mandy the way you did?"

Tonia got herself up and dusted off the snow on her outfit. "Ford, I was only trying to protect you. I saw her as a threat to you." Tonia inched closer. "I had no intention of killing her."

"Yeah? What about Lex and his friends, huh? Did you think Stin and I were going to let you get away with killing a bunch of teenagers? They're still *children.*" She bobbed her head. Ford could see the tears coming down her cheeks.

"I know Ford. I know the rules. I wouldn't hurt them. I'm sorry. Don't you understand? You were hurt. My first instinct will always be to protect you." She wiped her tears and sniffed. "Ford, she hurt you. You should have seen what she did to you. It was like she had no emotion about who she hurt."

Ford rammed his fingers through his hair.

"Tonia, she tried to stop it but she couldn't, that's what happens when you're transitioning. You of all people should remember that, you've been through it just as much as I have," Ford said. "Stin filled me in on what happened and you know what? I'm grateful Lex was there to stop her. If he weren't there, she probably would be dead."

"No. Not true Ford. I knew you cared about her. I told you I would never hurt you that way. Can't you see how much I—" Tonia cut herself off.

"I don't have time for this. I have to go find Mandy before she gets hurt or worse." With his back toward her, Ford grabbed the first Jet Ski he could find and got on.

"You don't even know where you're going. Do you have any idea where she is?" Before Ford could respond, Tonia continued. "I know where she is. I just happened to be outside when she and Lex were talking."

Ford jumped off the Jet Ski.

"Talking about what?" Tonia exhaled.

"Mandy was talking to Lex about apologizing to his father so they can go back home. She didn't think you were going to recover from the Binosil."
Ford grabbed Tonia's shoulders.

"What else did they say? Did they mention anything about a location?" Tonia shook her head.

"It wasn't a specific location. Lex pleaded with her to reconsider, saying that Vernon was dangerous to them both and that if they ever went back, he'd kill them."

"Location Tonia, I need to know where she went." Ford's grip was tighter around her shoulders than Tonia expected.

"You're hurting me." Ford loosened his grip. He couldn't play these guessing games with her. He needed to find Mandy and Lex.

"Look, Tonia, we're wasting time here. Mandy and Lex could be in serious danger right now, and all you're giving me is a load of bullshit. Just tell me what you know!"

Have to get out of here. Have to go find Mandy.

"They said something about it being cold all year long. Lex complained about how much he hated it there. The only place I could think of was—"

"—Alaska," Ford replied. There were some places in Alaska that were colder than others, but it was a start. Relief flooded through him. He hopped on the Jet Ski and started up the engine.

"I can help you find her Ford," Tonia said.

"No thanks. I can look for her on my own." With one swift turn, Ford blazed down the water and headed toward Alaska.

I will find you and bring you home…

***

"You can't be serious about this Mandy. He'll kill us both!"

"He won't kill you, Lex. Do you honestly think I would let him touch you?" Mandy asked.

"Mandy please, you have to turn this car around. I can't go back, I've failed him!" Lex pleaded. Mandy raised a brow but continued to keep her eyes on the road.

"You don't know the real reason why I was sent to the island Mandy. It wasn't because my father wanted me to have a better life." Mandy thought about his statement. A terrible feeling yanked inside her stomach.

It has to be true. Why would his own son say such a thing?

"So why did you come, Lex?" Mandy pushed the thought out of her mind and focused on the road. For this to work, she had to give Vernon a chance. After all, who was to say that the nightmares were real? She had lost her memory, which in turn caused her to forget her own husband.

"I came because Vernon wanted me to kill Ford. I was sent as some sort of hitman Mandy. He wanted me to kill Ford and the rest of the Truson Super Elite team because of the money."

"How?"

"By stealing their identities to have access to Ford's bank account. Vernon couldn't access yours because your parents froze your account after they suspected my father had something to do with your murder." The feeling started getting worse. Her alter ego pulled at her, wanting to come out and shield her from what Mandy was about to do. Mandy controlled her by removing her back inside but didn't know if she had the strength to do it again.

"Mandy, I'm telling you the truth. I never knew how the relationship was between you two. I was sent away to boarding school after my mother was killed. The only time I came to visit Dad was on spring break. That's when he announced the engagement. That was when we first met."

Mandy fell silent as Lex continued.

"I didn't want anything to do with my father after he killed my mother. He sent me back to boarding school after the wedding. I came back home when Vernon told me about your death. It was all a setup. He wanted me to come back home after he couldn't gain access to your money. That's when he told me I needed to kill Ford to stay in school. That's when he sent me here to the island. Tell me you remember Mandy." Mandy channeled her thoughts.

She tried to figure out if she had heard any conversation or seen anything that told her Lex was telling the truth.

It doesn't matter. Turn around and go back to the island. Ford needs your help.

"I'm sorry Lex, I don't remember." She paused. Her palms gripped the steering wheel. After her transformation from orca to human to get to Alaska, a stinging pain invaded her hands. She stopped driving when she reached the light and shook off the pain. It felt like she had driven for hours, but it was only a couple of miles. Thankfully, Vernon's home wasn't far away from where they were. Now all she needed to find was the house they used to stay in.

She couldn't remember where that was either.

It helped that Vernon was willing to cooperate after the horrible argument he and Lex had before Mandy managed to escape from the headquarters with a tote bag on her shoulder—everything she needed on the road until she was able to go back home. Home. That word didn't resonate with Vernon like she desired. Visions of Ford invaded her mind, the images of him lying in the hospital bed. Guilt flooded through her. If he wasn't going to recover…

"The light Mandy," Lex said, interrupting her thoughts.

"Thanks." She continued driving, peeking out of the side mirror to see if she could recognize the house Vernon described. He said something about a red house that had vines on it somewhere on a hill. She reminded herself to call him again once she found the nearest rest stop. She put on the turn signal at the next light. Before she turned, Lex grabbed the wheel.

"What are you doing?"

"I'm sorry Mandy. I can't let you go back to the way things were before. *I* can't go back to the way things were before." Mandy tried her best to jerk the wheel in her direction, but Lex was too strong. Mandy tried again. The wheel wouldn't move.

"Move your hands Lex!"

"No!" He replied. Lex gripped the steering wheel until Mandy heard the crunch of metal and watched as the wheel turned into stone. Mandy gasped. With her hands in mid-air, she turned her eye on Lex.

"Surprised?" When Mandy couldn't move, Lex decided to break the silence. "I don't know if you noticed, but I have powers just like Dad. The difference is my power is stone and boulders. My dad's powers are the same as yours."

"How…is…that…possible?" Mandy said. She exhaled and carefully placed her hands on her knees. "I was under the impression that the Truson S.E.T. were the only ones that knew."

Lex scoffed. He sat back in the recliner.

"Mandy, I found out so many things about my father and Samuel, it's ridiculous," Lex said. "I'm trying my best to protect you."

Mandy swallowed. "Protect me from what? Your father?"

"Yes, he's dangerous. Did you see how dangerous Samuel was? He sent an entire army to search for you once he found out you were alive. My father will be ten times worse than Samuel without blinking." Lex leaned toward Mandy again. "I can't let you go back there, Mandy. I don't want to see you hurt." Mandy stroked his cheek.

"I wouldn't let anything happen to you. You should know that—" Lex grabbed her hand.

"You're my stepmother Mandy." *Stepmother?* The word rang a bell. The music flowed softly into her thoughts. She saw herself in a wedding gown, taking baby steps to Vernon. She saw the smile etched on Vernon's face. Was this a memory? It had to be. The wedding gown, her so-called husband, greeting her from the aisle— it seemed like the most beautiful wedding she ever witnessed. She smiled. She wanted to hold on to that memory. That memory was the only thing keeping her from going back to Ford.

Could this be Vernon? Could this be the same man who abused me? She didn't know if Vernon was an abuser or not. In the nightmares she endured, she couldn't even see his face.

Stop making excuses.

Her alter ego roared in agreement.

"Mandy, are you all right? Is someone trying to contact you?" Lex put his hands on her shoulders and shook her. "Mandy, *talk* to me."

"I'm fine," she finally said. She stared out of the window as her mind wandered someplace else. "I think I may have had my first memory."

Lex shifted.

"Really? What did you remember?"

"A wedding. I think it was my wedding. I saw Vernon's face."

"What was he wearing?" Lex asked.

"He was wearing a pinstriped jacket and pants. He had a red handkerchief in his left pocket. His hair was all white and shiny like he just got his hair washed or something. He managed to put it in a ponytail."

Lex nodded.

"I was right, it's a memory?" Lex smiled. "That's a memory. I was there at the wedding. You're right." Mandy exhaled. A sense of relief flooded through her. She thought she would never get her memory back, that her memories would be nonexistent.

"What else do you remember?" Mandy tried to focus on anything else that came to mind, but nothing happened.

"All I remember is the wedding." *And all of the horrible nightmares I've suffered.* "Shut up!"

"Who are you talking to?" Lex looked out the window.

"Nobody." Mandy stared at the wheel. "We're not going to be able to go anywhere if the wheel is stuck like this. Can you work your magic and break it so we can go?"

"Under one condition." Mandy had a feeling she knew what that condition was. She *had* to move on. Despite whatever Vernon had done, she was his wife. They were married. That had to at least count for something.

"You can't go back to Vernon, I won't let you."

"If I don't go back to Vernon then where am I going to stay?"

"On the island," Lex said. "You have a better shot of being protected there than with Vernon. We both do." Mandy shook her head.

"That's not an option right now. I hurt Ford—"

"—It was an accident, Mandy. You didn't mean to hurt him. Your powers were out of control. You tried to stop it but you couldn't." A honk signaled behind them. Lex made a hand gesture to move around them. Apparently, the person got the message and walked beside them only to stop and roll the windows down.

"Uh…I don't know if you guys are new to this town, but we aren't very friendly when it comes to someone blocking the street," the man said.

Before Lex could speak, Mandy interrupted. "We're sorry. We're just a little lost—"

"What the—?" The man stared at the wheel. Mandy could tell he was confused by the reaction he gave out. "What happened to your car? Did somebody do this?" A stinging pain etched through Mandy's brain. With every breath she took, the pain escalated.

Tell Lex to undo it. That voice. She knew who it was. How the hell did he get inside her mind? She wasn't underwater…

Never mind that. Tell Lex to undo it…now!

"Are you all right madam?" The guy asked, peeking into the window.

"She's fine," Lex barked. "Look, there's nothing for you to see here. Can you please leave us be?" The man was about to comment but didn't have the opportunity to do so. A figure came up from behind the backseat of his car and grabbed his neck. Mandy saw flashes of lightning shooting from his eyes, his body convulsing like a madman.

Tell Lex to undo it Mandy! Tell him now!

Panic sent shockwaves through her. She gripped the steering wheel. A massive surge of electricity sprung through her hands, causing the stone to crumble onto her feet. Though the stones were heavy, she pushed the accelerator and sped down the street without stopping.

"We need to find someplace safe. I don't know who that was, but after what I saw, I don't think I want to find out." Mandy saw Lex staring at the back window but kept her eyes on the road.

"What? What do you see?" Mandy asked.

"We're in trouble."

Mandy made a swift turn at the end of the street and kept speeding.

Pay attention, Mandy. I want you to find the nearest place you two can hide for the next few hours.

"Mandy, look out!"

Mandy stopped the car. She stared at the skinny blue-haired woman as she reached out her arm. The unknown woman bent her fingers into her palm. Mandy thought about the shield Ford had taught her before the woman was able to turn the entire car to pieces. Electrical lines shot out from her knuckles causing the windshield to break.

Mandy's powers connected with the woman's and exploded. The woman flew in mid-air and ended up hitting a light pole before her body slammed into the street. Two cars skidded on the gravel to avoid her. Mandy put the car in reverse, turned and sped off, the car going in the opposite direction.

"It's not going to work Mandy. It's too late now, they found us," Lex said.

"What are you talking about?" Mandy paused. "Lex, do you know them?"

Lex nodded.

"Yeah, I know them. They're the goons who used to work for Samuel. They must have found out about Samuel's death."

"I thought we killed them all?" Mandy asked. "There was no one left standing on the island after the battle was done."

"That doesn't mean anything when it comes to the Transforments." Lex stared at the person blocking them. He walked toward them, his face becoming more revealing by the second. Lex slammed his head against the seat.

"We're dead."

CHAPTER FOURTEEN

Ford tried contacting Mandy after the first thoughts went through. He had to admit it was difficult for him to use mind control considering how little the team handled it when they were human. He knew it was successful when she started asking questions about how he got inside her mind.

Did she listen? He wasn't sure.

Despite his efforts, he still couldn't pinpoint the location of where they were. All he saw was a road and some grass covered in snow. He had to rely on his instincts, something he used quite often when it came to thinking on his feet. He pushed the brakes on his Jet Ski to slow down when he reached land. The Jet Ski came to a complete halt and crashed into the muddy ice water while Ford got off and surveyed the area.

The sky was dark—way too dark—to see much of anything. *There probably wouldn't be any streetlights for a while.* Ford pulled out his flashlight and continued walking until he saw the sign "Welcome to Alaska." Relief flooded through him. He felt as if he was in the right place but needed to check.

He took out his cell and dialed the number to the Truson Headquarters. After three rings, he heard Su-Lee's voice on the other end.

"Truson Headquarters, this is Su-Lee, how may I help you?"

"Su-Lee, this is Ford. I need you to do me a favor."

"Ford? The last time I heard from you was—never mind. I'm always the last person to find out anything around here." Su-Lee exhaled. "Okay, what's the favor?"

"I need you for you to search the last location Vernon was in before the accident.

"Are you near a computer right now?"

"You know me, Ford. I didn't become a computer whiz for nothing. I'm *always* at my computer doing something," Su-Lee said.

Ford heard the sound of the keyboard as Su-Lee began to type away. He continued walking. He felt the snow getting denser with each step. There were a couple of houses in the distance, but he wasn't sure which one belonged to Vernon. He grunted. He should have planned this out more carefully.

"Got it!"

"Where is he?" Ford asked, anticipation gnawing at him. He needed to be with Mandy to make sure she and Lex were okay. *Doubt that's going to happen.*

"He's in Fairbanks. Surprisingly, he's been there for a while. He's staying in a red cabin a few miles from where you're walking right now, and before you ask the million-dollar question of how I know where you are, you're not the only one who knows how to pick other people's thoughts, mister."

Ford didn't bother to respond.

"What's the address?" Su-Lee recited the address. Ford kept repeating it to himself.

"Why don't I send a text message so you won't be so busy repeating it?"

"That's better," Ford said. He needed to focus on moving forward and trying to find the house.

"Okay, I'll text it to you." Once they hung up, Ford heard the noise on his cell. He stared at the address only to notice something catching his eye in the distance. He saved the text to his phone and walked closer. He couldn't make out exactly what it was until he stopped and stood a few inches away from it.

A car.

He sprinted toward it. He sniffed the air. It smelled like burnt metal and rubber. Chills went down his spine. Something wasn't right. Ford heard a crunch under his boots and squinted. He lifted his leg and saw tiny pieces of glass sticking to the sole. He peeled a piece of glass from the rubber and studied it carefully. The glass tore through his finger. He turned around.

The windows had been shattered to pieces, leaving a decoration of glass all over the road. Ford searched inside. None of the seats bared anything that resembled a struggle between any of them. The steering wheel said otherwise. It looked like somebody beat it to death.

She has to be okay. Both of them have to be okay.

Ford opened the driver's side of the car and found what looked to be stone on the pedals. Fear clenched his chest. They must have been in danger—why else would Lex use his powers?

Have to find them fast!

Ford poked his head out of the car and slammed the door. He scurried away only to find a dead body. Ford's boots crunched against the snow, picking up the pace until he finally keeled over and examined the body. Ford took his fingers and carefully turned the head.

A woman.

Not Mandy.

Relief flooded through him while he tried to identify the woman. A part of him didn't really care, but he needed to know if this unnamed woman had an ID. From the way it looked, he could only predict what happened next between Lex, Mandy and her. He patted her down and checked her pockets—nothing. Ford stood and grabbed his cell out of his pocket, took a picture of the young woman's face and sent it to Su-Lee for information.

He stared at the symbol on her arm. It depicted a black circle with two heads sticking out of it. One represented an orca, the other a man. Ford tried to remember where the symbol came from. As he concentrated, Su-Lee's text popped up on his cell.

"She's a part of the Transforments. I'm not sure what exactly happened, but my guess would be they were kidnapped. When I looked up the location of where Vernon was, I also found his army lurking around the surrounding area."

The phone rang after that. Ford answered.

"Yeah, what else do you have Su-Lee?"

"Do you need back up for this mission?"

"No, thank you…"

"Ford, I know you're probably upset at us for letting her get away, but can we please just put those feelings aside right now and focus on coming together as a team? There's a possibility you could be outnumbered here, and I don't want a repeat of what happened—" Su-Lee got cut off when someone grabbed his phone from behind and started talking. Ford flinched and shifted his gaze to the man standing behind him.

"I'm sorry *Orman*, it seems like we're having a bad connection right now. I'm afraid Ford will have no other choice but to talk to you in another life." The man turned and sneered at Ford. "Or maybe not." He dropped the phone on the ground and crushed it with his foot.

"Who are you?" Ford asked. His alter ego gripped inside him, ready for an attack.

"I'm one of Vernon's many associates. He's been expecting you by the way." The guy stepped closer. Ford balled his fists. His hands were burning. *Got to get it together until I find them.* "Would you like to come with me and see your lovely mistress and her spoiled stepson?"

"Take me to them. Where are they?" Ford barked. He felt the flames shooting out of his hands. The unnamed man cocked his head to the side.

"If you want to see them, I'm afraid you must find a way to control your temper." Ford grimaced at his comment but held himself back for Mandy and Lex's sake.

Apparently, this man was the key to finding them, and Ford needed to do just that before Vernon got the chance to harm them.

"My temper *is* controlled. I want to see them…take me to them or else you're going to see what it's really like when I'm angry."

The man shrugged. "Very well. Follow me."

***

The chains dug into Mandy's delicate skin as she trudged through the snow with Lex by her side. She shot him a look, hoping she would see how he felt when it came to her decision to go back to Vernon. But Lex never noticed her once, never lifted his head in her direction. He stared at his feet the entire time. Mandy knew he had to be pissed about the whole thing.

She wouldn't have blamed him if he never spoke to her again.

"Keep it movin' you two, we're almost there," one of Vernon's goons said.

"We're going as fast as we can. It would really help if you unhooked these chains," Mandy said. The two men laughed at her.

"Nice try lady. We know what you're trying to do. We're not stupid." The men shoved her again.

"Hey, would you relax? We're doing what you asked us to do," Lex said. The man jerked the chains on his wrist and shoved him around.

"We call the shots here boy, not you."

"Enough!"

Mandy and Lex focused on the sound of the voice before they realized who it was. The man had white hair pulled back in a ponytail. He was dressed in a red suit with black shoes and a black tie.

"If anyone is going to torture them, it's going to be me."

Torture? Not what she was hoping. She wanted a happy homecoming, not one where she and Lex would have to fear for their lives. If only she could find some way out of this fiasco…

Somehow, she doubted it was going to happen.

The man stepped forward until he was inches from Lex. The more Mandy stared at him, the more Mandy remembered him. A chill crept up her spine as the white-haired man touched Lex's face. Mandy's alter ego gave out a warning.

"My son, all I ever wanted was for you to follow my orders so we could become the most powerful and wealthiest team on the planet. For that to happen, you needed to get rid of the one person who I despised more than anyone else."

"Ford Mayfield," Lex responded. The man smiled.

"Yes. All you had to do was kill him and this would have been all over."

No! Her mind screamed. *You can't kill him.*

"No! It's not true. Lex, tell me it's not true?" Mandy waited for him to respond but had a feeling she wasn't going to like the answer. Her stomach clenched. Lex turned to face her with a mixture of sadness and anger. He had been through enough already and didn't need to suffer anymore.

Neither did Ford.

She wanted Ford to come and wrap his protective arms around her and tell her everything was going to be okay. She wanted him to shield her and Lex from whoever this man was and destroy anyone who got in the way of rescuing them. She tried to do that herself— the problem was the goons who were hired by Vernon ordered them to strip away their powers as soon as they found them.

"But you couldn't, could you? You couldn't be man enough to follow my orders."

Follow my orders. Mandy repeated the words in her head. His voice…those words…sounded so familiar…A grainy vision of the same man invaded her mind. The images were blurry at first but eventually came into focus.

She gasped.

"I'll never follow through with your orders *Dad*," Lex said. "You always wanted me to do stuff I wasn't comfortable with. I just wanted to be a normal kid—hang out with some of my old friends, get schoolwork done so I could graduate, those kinds of things." Vernon smirked.

"Do you honestly think you were going to be something in life considering the condition you have? Who would want to deal with somebody like you, son?" Mandy's alter ego stirred again. She didn't like where this conversation was going. Was this really the famous husband she married?

"I mean, look at you. You're white as a ghost. You can't even go out in the sun without covering yourself up." Mandy shifted her weight.

"How can you talk to your son that way? Don't you care about him at all?" Vernon shifted from Lex to her. With his hands directly behind his back, Vernon stood tall and straight and gave out a sly grin.

"Hello, *wife.*"

Was that sarcasm etched in his voice?

"I actually thought I was going to get away with it, but I guess you are just too smart for your own good, huh?"

"What are you talking about?" Mandy asked. Another vision passed through her mind. This time, she pictured herself in a car sitting next to Vernon. Vernon clapped his hands together causing the vision she had to fade.

"That's right my love. You don't remember anything, do you?" Vernon caressed her cheek with his thumb. She thought the gesture would reassure her she was safe. It only made her tense.

"Yes, I do."

Vernon raised a brow.

"Really? That's interesting. The last comment I heard from my associates was you couldn't remember anything. You couldn't remember your own name."

"Well, I can," Mandy said. "I'm better now." The other associates hovered and had their own silent conversation after that announcement. Mandy didn't care at this point. She really wanted Ford to come and save her from this intolerable position. Why didn't she listen to Lex when he told her to turn and go back to the island?

Not time for regrets now. Think Mandy. How are you going to get Lex out of this?

"So, if you're so much better, why haven't you tried contacting me sooner? I am your husband after all." He paused. "You do remember, don't you?"

"Yes, I remember." Vernon squinted, and Mandy wondered what was going through his mind while she fiddled with the chains around her wrists. She kept telling herself it was her husband, that he would do whatever he could to protect her. The more she thought about it, the more her body tensed.

"And what exactly do you remember wife?" Vernon crossed his arms, waiting for her answer.

"Maybe she would tell you if you ushered us inside the house and unhooked us from these chains. My body has had enough of the cold weather, and I'm pretty sure my stepmother is cold and hungry as well," Lex said. "Can we go inside?" Vernon smirked. Anger boiled inside her.

"I guess I can arrange that for you." Vernon spun on his heel. "Come with me please." Mandy and Lex followed closely behind. They turned their heads every so often to see if the guards would do something to trigger a response from Vernon.

Nothing.

Mandy didn't realize how incredibly cold her body had become until she stepped inside the house. She basked in the warm glow as the heat radiated through her skin.

Her eyes roamed the room. The living room was small compared to the living room at Ford's cabin. As they stepped inside, she noticed a red love seat and an old TV that looked like it came from the 1950s. She closed her eyes and tried to see if she could remember anything—a memory, a dream—something that represented her past.

Nothing.

"Take off the chains!" Vernon ordered. Two of the guards obeyed the request and fumbled with the chains. Mandy heard them drop to the floor and finally moved her arms.

"So, when are we going to get our powers back, Dad? Or are you keeping it for us to suffer under your misery?" Lex asked, rubbing his wrists.

"You haven't seen the meaning of suffering yet, son." Vernon strolled into the living room and made himself cozy by sitting on the love seat. Mandy and Lex sat down on the couch while the two guards stood behind Vernon.

"I think it's time for us to catch up first before I finally give the last blow to both of you."

Lex shrugged.

"What happens now? Are you the new leader of Samuel's group? Do you honestly think this so-called partnership between you and Samuel's goons is going to last because Samuel's gone?" Silence filled the air before Lex picked up the conversation again. "You're wrong. These goons are only working for you because they have no choice."

"Yes, and you want to know why their leader is gone? It's because of the Truson Super Elite Team. They managed to destroy the one leader I admired and respected all these years."

Mandy hung back on the couch and tried concentrating on what she could remember about the place or why she was uneasy about the whole situation.

Simple. The man is going to kill you and Lex.

"You didn't admire and respect Samuel. I've heard many conversations where you wanted to get rid of him. I'm not stupid, Dad." A flash of anger burned within him.

Mandy shivered. This wasn't going to end well.

Think, think, think.

"All right, there may have been a couple of times where I've wanted to get rid of him—"

"—You wanted to get rid of him just like you got rid of my mom and Mandy."

Mandy jerked her head and gaped at him. What was he talking about? Dammit, why couldn't she remember anything about Vernon and the life they shared together? "The only difference was you didn't succeed with Mandy. Mandy survived because of Ford and his team. So how does it feel to be outsmarted by your own wife?"

Vernon stood up and grabbed Lex by the neck.

Time for action.

With all the weight she had, Mandy tackled Vernon to the ground. The other two guards quickly intervened by rushing to help their fallen leader. With no time to waste, Mandy grabbed Vernon by the neck and started choking him. Vernon somehow managed to get the upper hand by pushing her back against the wall.

"Mandy!"

Sparks shot throughout her body. Not having her powers to protect herself from Vernon's damage knocked the wind out of her. She had to get up and move. She couldn't end her life this way…

Her body continued to lie still while she watched Lex and Vernon's goons tackle each other on the living room floor…

***

Kick. Punch. Kick. Punch. Kick, punch, crack.

That was all Lex heard and felt as he delivered blow after blow to Vernon's bodyguards. He wanted his alter ego to come out blazing but knowing he was nowhere near the water, he fought his best to control the emotions going through his body while trying to fight the bodyguards at the same time. Once he got the two bodyguards down, he searched for the one who took his powers away.

"I must say, you're very strong even without your powers," his father said. "I didn't think you had it in you to take them down."

"Just like you thought I didn't have it in me to take you down too." Before Vernon spoke, Lex cut him off. "Don't bother giving me a speech on how awful I am because of my skin. I'd rather not hear it."

Vernon whistled, and the close proximity between them made Lex want to beat him senseless.

He was tired of being the son his father never wanted. He'd tried to do everything he could to please him. Lex scoffed. What was the point of it all? This whole experience felt like a waste of time—time he could have spent having fun being a kid and spending time with his friends. Instead, he was here protecting the woman he adored since they first met a year ago. He didn't mind doing it, he just wanted his father destroyed and to move on with his life.

He couldn't do that until he killed his father.

"It's fascinating. You two really think you can beat me. I've been here longer than you have. I have more powers than you could ever imagine." Vernon stepped closer. "Do you know how easy it is to get rid of you?"

"Not easy enough," Lex said. Vernon raised his fist. The guards scrambled to grab Lex away from Vernon, but Vernon stopped them by raising his other hand.

"Don't bother. I'm going to love seeing him suffer after the way he's treated me." With one good swipe across the face, Lex fell back and landed hard on the dark blue carpet beneath him.

CHAPTER FIFTEEN

Ford was just coming up to the door when he saw a bunch of men scrambling inside the house. One of the guards had led him to the place where he wanted to be and just before the commotion started, he ditched one of them by grabbing him and setting his neck on fire. He died instantly. More Transforments began rushing in to help, but Ford kept them in check by using his powers to eliminate them.

By the time he was done, nearly a dozen Transformments were on the snow in agonizing pain. It was one of those times where he loved being the boss of the Truson Super Elite Team.

As the men rushed inside, Ford did his best to blend in with the crowd. It didn't take him long to find Vernon and Lex going at each other's throats. Unfortunately, Vernon was winning by a thread. Ford stepped into the action, shooting a fireball at Vernon that sent the man flying through the wall. His focus then turned to the guards. He felt a knot in his stomach.

Where was she?

He started to fight every person that came to his view. He thought it might have been two or three rushing to help their fallen leader but after six or seven men came bursting through the doors wanting a piece of him and Lex, he decided it was time to call the other members of the group. He pictured Stin and the others in his mind, hoping to communicate with them the same way he interacted with the team when they were underwater.

Su-Lee, Stin, Tonia and Gabriel, I need you. We're in trouble, and we need your help.

Just when he thought the fight was over, more of Vernon's men came out of hiding and started throwing electric balls, stones, small tornadoes and anything else they could find at Ford. He let himself get distracted by focusing on Lex who seemed to be losing the battle. *Where was Mandy?* The fact that she wasn't coming to Lex's rescue proved something was wrong. Ford tried to strengthen his power as much as he could by destroying the enemy at a faster speed than average.

Almost there.

Ford searched for Mandy after what he'd hoped was the last of the Transforments. He quickly surveyed all of the bodies that were either dead or injured before he ran to the aid of Lex who he saw slouched in the corner of the hallway.

"Lex." Ford shook him. Nothing. "Lex? Lex, look at me. Open your eyes!" Ford shook him again. Nothing. Panic rose in his throat. *He can't be dead.*

"Lex." With one closed fist, Ford socked Lex in the face, hoping his worst fears wouldn't come to light. His plan worked. Ford was relieved when Lex let out an "Ow" and rubbed his jaw.

"What did you do that for?" he whined. "I'm going to have a broken jaw!"

"Be lucky I saved your life. If it wasn't for me punching you out, I don't think you were going to make it." A small grin etched across Ford's face before it faded again. "Do you know where Mandy is? Is she here?"

Lex nodded. "There's a problem though."

"What happened?"

Lex twitched his jaw. A bruise started to form on his cheek. Didn't make sense to him. He was one of the Transforments. Why wasn't Lex able to heal right away?

"One of the Transforments stole both Mandy's and my powers on the way here. They told us they needed to do it so we wouldn't try anything with them." Visions of Mandy being defenseless against Vernon's horrible goons cascaded through Ford's brain.

"Do you know if he's still here? Do you remember what he looks like?"

"I never forget a face," Lex said. Lex described the man's features to Ford.

Ford wasted little time walking around the bodies until he found who he was searching for. He grabbed his neck and felt the dead man's energy flow through him like a maze, zigzagging every possible vein and organ it could find until the man was unresponsive. Throwing him down on the floor, Ford grabbed Lex by the arm and put his hand on his chest.

"This might hurt a bit, but I think you'll feel a lot better afterward," Ford said. The powers flowed from Ford to Lex within seconds. It took a while for Lex to feel the energy through his veins. He gasped and fell to the floor. He blinked a couple of times while Ford stooped over and extended his hand to help Lex up.

"Thanks," Lex said.

"No problem. Let's go find Mandy." Ford inspected the hallways and opened up the bedrooms for any signs of her. The more they looked, the more nervous he became. His stomach dropped when he entered the third bedroom and couldn't find her.

"Where is she? Do you know what happened to her?" Lex shrugged.

"She was in battle with me and Vernon. She saved my life just a few minutes ago. If it weren't for her, I would be dead."

"It's great you feel that way, but we need to find her before Vernon does."

"Did someone call me?" a familiar voice asked.

Lex and Ford stared at each other before they decided to follow where the voice came from. They carefully walked into the dining room area and surveyed the light brown tables and chairs centered in the middle of the room. Lex and Ford inched closer. Ford's alter ego roared with fury when he saw Mandy sitting in a chair surrounded by an electric tightrope.

Lex and Ford lurched forward to try and rescue Mandy from Vernon's clutches.

"I wouldn't do that if I were you. If you touch her, the current will bounce off of you and reflect back to Mandy, which will kill her indefinitely," Vernon said. Ford let out a snarl. His powers started building inside his chest. His alter ego wanted to rip Vernon to shreds.

No one touches her except for me.

"Dad, why are you doing this? Why are you making our lives miserable?"

Vernon laughed. It sent chills through Ford's spine. Images of Vernon pulling the handle down on the explosives causing the Jet Ski to explode into a million pieces sifted through his mind.

"You really want to know the answer to that question, don't you?" He leaned his head to the side, never taking his eyes off of Lex.

"Yes, I do. I don't get it. I don't get why you would want to kill me or your wife to get what you want," Lex said. Vernon shrugged.

"Well son, I would be more than happy to tell you about why I want Mandy to disappear from this earth. I could say it's about the money, but that would only be half-true." He carefully put one step in front of the other and put his hands in his pockets. Ford's hands curled into fists. He wanted to kill him. He knew that if he let his alter ego out, he would surely die because of the lack of water supply. Ford stared at Mandy, and his heart nearly ripped into pieces.

"The real reason is because of our history—me and Ford. Isn't that right, Ford?" A wink and a smile made Ford's insides stir. A surge of energy went through him. He was getting close to losing it.

"You need to release her now! If you don't, I will make sure you leave this earth and are never reborn again!"

"Ugh!" Vernon slammed the chair down onto the floor. The backside crumbled to pieces. "Why do you always do that? Why do you always have to give your stupid demands and interrupt my story, huh?"

"It's okay," Mandy said from across the room. "Just from sitting here for what seems like an eternity, I think I've finally figured out what happened."

Ford lifted a brow.

"What do you mean? I'm confused," Lex said. Mandy tried to relax her shoulders in the chair, but it didn't work. Without her powers, she wouldn't be able to protect herself from the electrical current surrounding her. One wrong move and she was gone for sure.

"The memories—I remember what happened. I remember everything. There were good experiences between Lex and me and not-so-good experiences between me and Vernon." She paused as she reflected on what she remembered. "I tried to understand why he would abuse me so much, but I never knew why."

Ford's chest tightened. Mandy abused? How long did she suffer at the hands of this monster? Never again.

"Oh, there's a reason why." Vernon moved closer to Mandy until their faces were only a few feet apart. "You weren't the woman I was supposed to have. You were a rebound, just someone I wanted to screw around with."

"Get away from her, I'm warning you," Ford said through clenched teeth. He tried to calm himself down, but his alter ego wanted otherwise. Vernon turned on his heel and shrugged.

"It's such a shame I can't even tell my own wife my darkest secrets without you interfering. How rude can you possibly be?"

"I've done this long enough. I'm so sick and tired of you playing the innocent victim in all of this, Dad. You're not innocent, you never were. You wanted to kill Mandy just like you killed Mom," Lex said.

Ford squinted.

"Your mother was just like Mandy—a whore. She slept with everyone and everything that ever crossed her path." Heat throbbed at Ford's neck. He could tell the urges were there—that feeling of his powers coming to the surface was evident—but it felt a little different. He felt stronger…

He couldn't contain his powers for too much longer…

Ford suddenly felt a flash of wind. He saw Lex form a boulder small enough to hoist at his father. It never succeeded. Vernon wasted little time attacking Lex by planting a power move of his own. The flow of electricity slammed Lex against the table, knocking both him and Mandy to the floor.

Eyes burning. Heart racing. Mind suffocating. Flashes of Roxanne came to him. A gigantic surge of electricity plummeted Ford's body. He launched himself at Vernon, his touch deadlier than the first. A mixture of fire and electricity gripped into Vernon's skin, his arms laced with third-degree burns before Vernon managed to punch

Ford in the jaw. The orange and blue glow cascading around them faded out, blending in with the lights of the chandelier.

Another surge, this time the powers of electricity jolted out from Ford's body and into Mandy's chest.

"Mandy!" Lex screamed. Ford tried to concentrate on what was happening but couldn't. His powers were strong—too strong—to focus on anything.

Can't control it.

Ford's temperature shifted from hot to cold within a matter of seconds. The bitter air flared into his nostrils, his body a frozen icicle.

Stin had arrived.

He quickly felt himself losing energy due to extreme weather changes. Ford focused on Vernon before both of them collapsed onto the floor, and Vernon coughed a couple of times before he gained control of his breathing.

"You, all of you, make me sick. All I wanted was Roxanne. I wanted to be happy and live a happy, normal life with the woman I truly loved, and all you did was take her away from me," he spat.

"But what about me? Didn't you love me too?" Mandy asked, her voice cracking. Ford grimaced.

"How could I ever possibly love someone like you? You will never be Roxanne. The *only* reason why I married you was because of your money." Ford saw Mandy's expression change. He wondered what was going through her mind as he said those words. He certainly knew what was going through his.

Enough was enough. Ford needed to end it.

***

You're a whore. The only reason why I ever married you was for your money. Those word radiated through her brain like a tape recorder. It was at that pivotal moment that she remembered everything.

The slap across her face every time she disagreed with him on something…the punches and kicks he shared every time he was angry…She even remembered that night Vernon tried to kill her by running the car off the road and dumping it into the cold waters of the Arctic sea. And to actually think she'd wanted to come back home to him? What had she been thinking?

Anger burned through her. How dare he say those things to her after everything she'd done for him? She tried to be the best wife possible for him, but he still didn't appreciate her.

"It's time we end this Vernon. You have no more leverage. Your army is gone. You might as well surrender to us and let us arrest you and take you to trial, so you can stand in front of our ancestors and explain yourself."

Vernon scrambled to get up. He put his hand on the wall to steady himself.

"I don't need to do anything except destroy you for ruining my plans! None of this would have happened if Ford had backed off and let me and Roxanne have the life we'd always wanted!" He seethed.

"Roxanne never loved you, Vernon. She didn't see you that way, and you couldn't deal with it. We were husband and wife, that's it—end of story."

Vernon sprang off the wall and lunged at Ford.

You won't kill anyone else…not this time.

While the fight escalated between them, Mandy saw the electric belt fade away from her hands and waist. A blast of electricity went through her chest and flooded through her veins. She focused her attention on Lex who offered a smile, indicating that he was the one who gave her the power to defeat Vernon.

"Focus…Concentrate," Lex said.

Mandy closed her eyes and thought about Ford struggling under Vernon's power, trying to grab hold of what little strength he had left to fight for the people he loved…

Her powers started building, each strain of electricity striking her everywhere. The urge to fight was so intense she could barely hold herself together. As she held her hand back, a gust of wind distracted her. She could hear thunder rumbling outside. Windows suddenly cracked, spreading all of the glass onto the dining room floor.

"What the hell is going on?" Mandy heard Stin ask the team. Mandy smiled as the tornado burst through the house.

"Take cover!" she said. She immediately felt guilty about unleashing her power on her new team but knew she didn't want her husband to escape again.

"Freeze it!" Ford said. Stin nodded once and shot a stream of snow and ice out of his hands, creating a large sparkly statue of electricity and snow.

Vernon scoffed.

"Is this truly the best you can do? I can do better."

"I think not." Mandy's grin widened as Vernon formed a lightning ball in his hand and threw it at the tornado. The tornado created a mixture of ice and electricity and threw the ball back at Vernon, hitting him in the chest. Everyone went silent and didn't move until Vernon's body exploded into bits and pieces on the hardwood floor. Mandy took a deep breath. She hadn't realized she'd been holding it in for so long.

It was over. The memories of her past exploded. She asked herself what her true feelings were about the whole situation. There was only one word that popped up in her mind—relief. Mandy felt something leaning across her back. The touch awakened her out of the misery she remembered and put her back into the present.

"Mandy, are you okay?"

She shook her head and stared at the people who were partly responsible for giving her a second chance at life. She briefly reflected on Dr. Madison for her hard work and dedication bringing her to this moment…

"Yeah, I'm fine. I just realized you were right. The so-called husband I thought I loved ended up being such a disappointment," she said, never taking her eyes off Ford. He rubbed her shoulders.

"I'm sorry you had to remember the horrible things he did to you," he said. "How about we get out of here and go home—to our *real* home."

Mandy smiled. *Home.* Her new place was the island of Truson. Her new life as a true Orman had now begun.

Despite the excitement of her being a member of the Truson Super Elite Team, there was a sense of uneasiness she felt when it came to her and Ford. During this whole adventure, Ford never really expressed how he felt about her. Sure, they shared a kiss or two but considering everything that had happened, she never had a chance to think about how things would turn out.

Until now.

"Hey, I have an idea you guys are going to love. Why don't we all go to our favorite spot and celebrate?" Stin shrugged and waited for a response.

"What favorite spot?" Mandy asked, desperate to get her mind off of Ford. Maybe being around her newfound family and getting to know them would take her mind off of things for a little bit. She needed to relax after the day she'd had.

"It's called Nise's Bar and Grill. We chill out after a hard day at work. It's also the place where Stin nailed Nise when they first met," Su-Lee said. Stin's mouth dropped. He focused on Su-Lee's comment while the rest of the team started laughing. She smiled and wrapped her arms around Mandy's shoulders.

"Mandy, after your performance today, I think we should make you an official member of the Truson Super Elite Team. What do you say?"

"Sounds great," Mandy said with a smile. She searched all of the faces as they smiled and nodded their approval. All except the one person who had been giving her hell ever since she first met her.

Here's to her life being easier…

Her forming some sort of truce with Tonia heavily weighed on her mind as Tonia stepped forward and cleared her throat.

"Can I have everyone's attention?" Mandy heard Tonia's voice amidst the crowd of anxious members eager to get started on the celebration. *Should I help her?*

Mandy's initial reaction would have been no. After all the hell she had been put through, why should she help Tonia out with anything? But after seeing Tonia struggling for the next few seconds, she decided to give in. She placed her fingers into her mouth and whistled. Everyone stopped and focused their attention on Mandy.

"Uh, I think Tonia has something she would like to say," Mandy said. She stepped back and let Tonia have the floor.

"I know everyone's a little excited about our newest member of our team—"

"—Except you," Stin piped in. "You don't seem to be particularly overjoyed that Mandy's going to be a part of the new team."

"Will you please let me speak?" She paused. Mandy waited for some sort of comeback, but Stin remained silent. "I get that everyone's excited about Mandy being the new member of the team. But let us not forget the one factor that would make this all complete."

"Great Tonia, leave it to you to spoil a good moment."

"Cut it out Stin!" Su-Lee barked. "I want to hear what Tonia has to say. You can either shut up or get out."

"I second that notion," Ford interjected. Mandy nodded and stepped forward. If she wanted to mend fences between the members of her team, she had to let bygones be bygones and try to forgive Tonia for the things she'd done.

What a way to put on your big girl panties.

"Thank you, Su-Lee and Ford. Since the rest of you don't want to hear what I have to say—" Tonia glared at Stin before she continued—"I won't be too long. I just wanted to remind everyone that Dr. Madison is no longer here and that we need to find another member, an ancestor maybe—who can perform the Truson ceremony so we can make it official," Tonia said. She stared down at the floor before she decided to raise her hand.

"I say yes to the ceremony," Tonia announced. "I think that despite everything that happened between us, she would make a great member of the team."

Mandy expected her to at least give her a handshake after the speech. Instead, Tonia went back to her spot, gave a quick glance at Ford and shifted her weight. Soon, all of the members raised their hands.

"I agree."

"Me too."

"Third," Ford agreed. Ford rubbed Mandy's shoulders. "There's nothing I would love more than for her to stay where she belongs." A burst of energy flowed through her, and a new wave of emotions cascaded through her body all at once. The feeling overwhelmed her.

She tried to focus on something else and noticed Lex leaning against the wall with his head down. Mandy didn't even see the members cheering as she made her way through the crowd and came face-to-face with her stepson.

CHAPTER SIXTEEN

Echoes of members cheering for Mandy made his brain pop. He was more than happy that Mandy had a new family to love and honor for the rest of her second life. He stiffened when he saw Ford embrace Mandy. He wouldn't be surprised if those two fell in love and started raising a family of their own.

Without him.

Since Vernon had disappeared from his life and knowing the Transforments would never rise to the surface again, the question still remained where he was going to be after this was over. It had only been a couple of days since he first walked on the island with a deadly mission—to kill the members of the Truson S.E.T.

How things had changed.

He never expected to have any friends at the Truson School for Shapeshifters in such a short time, but he did. He never had friends back at his old school because of what he looked like. He was surprised when he met two guys from this school who never questioned the color of his skin. He finally felt like he belonged somewhere.

Now that feeling was over.

He had nowhere else to go. Both of his parents were dead. After the battle they had, Lex didn't have a home to go back to. Everything was destroyed.

"Lex?" A sweet melody aired into his ear. He didn't have to look at her to know who it was. "Lex? Are you okay?" He tried to smile so he could hide the feelings inside him. It was no use.

You might as well tell her the truth. There's no sense in hiding it anymore.

"I'm glad you're moving to the island," he said. "I think you're gonna like it here. Everyone seems to love you."

Mandy placed a hand on Lex's arm.

"And they are going to love you too. I'm not going back to the island without you," Mandy said. Lex took a step back.

"Thanks for the invitation Mandy, but I don't think I would be welcomed on the island after what happened with Ford. I could totally understand if they never wanted to see me again." It still didn't make it any easier for him to process. All he ever wanted was to be accepted into the world. He'd found that with his two friends. Lex saw Mandy shake her head.

"That's so not true. I don't think they are going to dismiss you in that fashion. I think forgiveness can be possible at this point since you didn't kill anyone. Besides, you were told what to do by Vernon. Vernon manipulated us all."

"She's right." Lex saw a pair of baby blues stare back at him. Stin. The teacher who took his cell and made his life difficult throughout his short journey. The man ultimately saved his life.

"Technically, you did nothing wrong. You could have followed through on your plan and killed every member of this team."

Lex shrugged.

"But you didn't. You had the power to kill anyone you wanted. With your kind of power, we would have been struggling to keep up with you." Lex raised a brow.

"Really?" Stin gave him a playful hit on the shoulder.

"Yeah, you have quite an aim. We would love to have you on our team. With Mandy, you and the rest of the team, we'll be unstoppable," Stin said.

Lex's eyes bulged. Him being a member of the Truson Super Elite Team? He reflected on how much he hated them at one point without ever understanding why. Maybe it was because of his dad's hatred for losing the only woman he ever loved—he didn't really know for sure. But he was about to be a part of something extraordinary.

Most importantly, he was going to be able to stay with his newfound friends no matter how much he wanted to punch them in the face sometimes.

"So, does this mean I don't need to go to school to become a member of the team?"

Stin shook his head.

"As part of the requirement for joining the team, everyone has to go through some sort of training before we officially swear you in as one of the newest members of the Truson S.E.T. Mandy needs to take some private lessons to control her powers." Lex shivered. He'd never forget the look Mandy had on her face when her powers took over. It looked like she was possessed.

He would die before that ever happened to him.

"Yeah, I totally get it," Lex said. He blocked the images from his mind. "But where am I gonna stay? Obviously, I can't stay here anymore, the place is a mess." Lex searched the whole room. Everything had been damaged in battle.

"We wouldn't leave you in this kind of condition." Stin snorted. "We wouldn't leave *anyone* in this sort of condition, human or otherwise."

He paused.

"You could come stay with me until everything has calmed down, right Mandy?"

Lex watched Mandy's expression. She smiled.

"I think if Lex is up for it, then I will have no problem with it as long as he stays on the island." Excitement surged through his veins. He couldn't believe it. He was going to stay on the island with his friends.

"It's official, you're in kid," Stin said. He rubbed Lex's head. Lex dug into his pockets to search for a cell.

"Oh yeah, can I have my cell back, please? I need to call all of my friends and tell them I'm not leaving." Stin rocked on his heels and stuffed his hands into his pockets. Mandy searched through her jeans and pulled out pieces of what was left of hers.

"I don't think we have any cellphones here. I think our powers destroyed them," Mandy said. Lex shrugged.

"It's okay. I'll surprise them. That way, they won't see me coming."

"Great idea," Ford said, interrupting the conversation. "Why don't you go get ready to head back to the island while I have a couple of words with Mandy." Lex saw the expression on Mandy's face. She looked horrified to be alone with him. Lex wondered what the problem could be as Stin lured him away from Mandy and walked him into the crowd of other members.

"C'mon Lex, I think it's time you met the other members of the team." Stin patted his shoulder and proceeded away.

***

Adrenaline cascaded through his veins. For the longest time, Ford tried to hide what he felt for her. He couldn't figure out how he could be so attracted to a woman after witnessing his dead wife lying in a coffin a decade ago. Now he wasn't so sure if he wanted to hide his feelings anymore.

"What is it you want to talk about?" Mandy asked.

What did he want to talk about? How happy he was about her staying? How much he wanted her to stay at his cabin and make love to her until he figured out what he finally wanted?

How unfair would that be?

"I'm glad that the members are letting you stay. I think you're going to love the ceremony."

"Thanks, that's very sweet of you to say," Mandy said. Silence filled the air. *Have to protect her. She has to stay with me.* Ford inched closer. After all the hell he went through, he couldn't let her walk out of the cabin and live somewhere else.

"Listen Mandy, if you want to stay at my cabin until the training is over, it's perfectly fine with me—"

"Ford?" Ford turned and stared at Tonia.

"Tonia, this is not a good time. I'm talking to Mandy right now. Can this wait?" How dare she pick this particular moment to interrupt what he had to say?

"I'm afraid it can't," she said. Her voice sounded shaky and a little off. He really didn't have time for any more of Tonia's emotional issues.

You're the leader. You have to handle this, or you might regret it later.

He silently protested as he stroked her cheek and studied her expression.

"I'm sorry, I have to see what she wants," he said. "Will you stay here until I return?" She removed his hand from her cheek and covered it with hers.

"I'm afraid not. It's been confirmed that Lex and I are both staying on the island, and Stin has invited Lex to stay with him." A knot formed in his throat.

"Have you asked him about you moving in as well?"

"Not yet." A sigh of relief flooded through his veins. Even his alter ego wasn't satisfied with that answer. "But I'm considering it, at least until I start getting the training I need to control my powers." She bit her nail. "I don't know what I'm going to do for money though."

"You automatically receive a paycheck when you start the training," Tonia said still focusing on Ford. "Ford, can I please talk to you? It won't take long."

Ford wanted to argue with Mandy about taking the deal. There was no way he would ever be okay with Stin and Mandy living together. He saw no reason why Lex and Mandy couldn't stay with him until she got settled. The thought of Stin spending so much time with his girlfriend and her stepson disturbed him.

He'd be damned if that happened.

"Ford, are you paying attention to me?" Tonia asked. He rubbed his eyes and pinched the tip of his nose.

"What is it, Tonia? What do you have to say to me that's so important?"

Tonia shifted her feet and started playing with her necklace before she stood still and fixed her gaze on him.

"I'm ready to apologize and explain the reasons why I did what I did." Ford folded his arms and watched Tonia exhale.

"I like the speech you gave about Mandy. I thought it was really nice," Ford said. Ford wanted to make the conversation as easy as possible so he could go back to Mandy.

"Thanks." Silence. "Well, I wanted to just say how sorry I am about what happened with Mandy. I never meant to hurt her, I just wanted to protect you—"

"I don't need protecting when it comes to her Tonia. I don't understand—" Tonia raised her hand.

"Stop, please. Can I just finish this?" Tonia asked. Ford opened his mouth to say something but decided against it.

"Now I've realized she's not really a bad person and that she really wasn't the one who wanted us to die, but I still don't want you and her—" She stopped.

"Me and her what Tonia?"

Tonia put her hair behind her ear.

"Together. I don't want you and her together. I think that this partnership you two have is not good for either one of you because I'm in love with you," Tonia blurted out. Ford unfolded his arms.

"I'm sorry, what did you say?" A smile formed on Tonia's face while all of the members gawked at them, surprised by the announcement Tonia made. Tonia strode up to Ford's face and buried it in her hands.

"Ford, I've been in love with you ever since I became a member of this group. There is nothing in this world I wouldn't do for you. I know I'm not supposed to fall in love with someone like you, but I think breaking the rules every once in a while is okay, don't you?"

Stin snorted. "Only if it relates to you," he said.

Su-Lee elbowed him in the arm and told him to be quiet. Ford's eyes searched the room. He tried to search for a response to the situation that would let her down easy without severing their ties as friends. His eyes made contact with Mandy's.

She squinted at him before she shook her head and strutted away.

"I'm sorry Tonia. I hope this doesn't change anything between us but—" he paused. What was the best answer he could give her? He didn't even know how he felt about Mandy. All he knew was that he couldn't lose her. "I just don't think of us in that way. I've always thought of you as a friend, nothing more."

Tears formed around Tonia's eyes. He wanted to comfort her and tell her he still adored her as a friend, but before he could open his mouth, Tonia raced out of the room.

"Tonia wait!" Ford shouted. He wanted to go after her and apologize but he couldn't. He took a step but felt a hand on his shoulder, blocking him from making contact.

"Don't. You already said enough. Let me go talk to her." Su-Lee put a gentle hand on Ford before she turned and went after Tonia. Ford did what Su-Lee asked him to do, even though it didn't feel right to stand there while Tonia's heart had shattered into a million pieces.

"What a way to knock her down gently bro," Stin said. He gave Ford a gentle shake. "She'll be all right. Just give her a little time." Ford shrugged. A part of him felt guilty about what happened, but he didn't want to lead her on either. Maybe Su-Lee was right, perhaps he just needed to stay away from her.

And maybe you need to go find Mandy and tell her how you feel.

"So, are you ready for the celebration? We're all going to Nise's Bar and Grill tonight—I'm hoping Mandy will show up considering how she's the life of the party at the moment." Stin inched closer to him. "Did you nail her yet?"

Ford jerked his shoulders back.

"Stin, I don't have time for this conversation. I have to go find Mandy." He pushed his way through the small crowd hell-bent on talking to her about everything under the sun. Before he made it out the door, he turned.

"Oh and by the way, Mandy and Lex will be staying at my place, not yours," Ford said.

***

I just thought of you as a friend, nothing more. The words kept gnawing at her. She was so sure Ford would be able to honestly see her the same way she saw him—her life mate. She couldn't understand it. Since Ford was assigned to her five years after his transformation, she's always felt she would be the one for him.

She couldn't believe his answer.

"Tonia!" A familiar voice rang out. Tonia continued to stare out into the ocean, tears streaming down her cheeks and neck. "Tonia, I know you're going through a hard time right now but please don't kill yourself!"

Tonia spun around, surprised by her response. Kill herself over a guy? Never.

Tonia was way smarter than that. As Su-Lee got closer, it only took her a moment to realize how deep the pain of unrequited love was. Tonia felt a hand on her shoulder before Su-Lee embraced her.

"I'm sorry. I know you wanted to have some sort of romantic future with him—"

Tonia waved her hand away.

"Please stop. I don't want to be reminded of it anymore. It was just a stupid crush that got out of hand, that's all." Silence fell between them.

"Did you mean what you said back there? I thought it was really nice of you to welcome Mandy into the group."

Tonia's eyes turned to Su-Lee.

"The only reason why I let Mandy in is because of Ford. I honestly thought I was protecting him from her and Vernon. I thought she would end up hurting him." She shook her head. How could she have been so foolish to believe he would pick her over Mandy?

"But she didn't. She lost her memory, Tonia. She reminds me of us when we first started here."

"Yeah, but she was married to a *murderer,* Su-Lee. A murderer who just so happened to be the same murderer who killed Ford's wife ten years ago! What person in their right mind would ever go back to someone like that?" Tonia exhaled and skimmed her fingers through her hair.

"Look Tonia, I get it. You're having a hard time with getting dumped by someone you've had a crush on for years, but you have to move on. Ford made his choice already. Now you have to make yours," Su-Lee said.

"I hope that means you will find other ways to entertain yourself besides stalking men for a living," Stin said.

Su-Lee groaned.

Tonia squinted. What the hell was this guy's problem? Did he get a kick out of stalking her?

"Stin, why are you here bothering Tonia? Can't you see we're having a conversation?"

"I agree." Tonia folded her arms across her chest. "If you're here to gloat about Ford not giving me the time of day, save your breath."

"I'm not here to gloat," Stin said. "Just wanted to find Mandy so we can all get the hell out of this damn place," Stin said. He shivered. "Everywhere I walk reminds me of Vernon and his crew. I can't take it." Stin walked past Su-Lee and headed in Tonia's direction. "I'm really sorry about Ford. I know how much you loved him."

Tonia swallowed. "Thank you," she said, surprised by his empathy. Tonia tried to remember the last time Stin had ever sympathized with her on anything. She came up with nothing.

"I'm going to load up some boats—or Jet Skis—so we can get back home," Stin said. Su-Lee raised a brow. Tonia's eyes widened. She knew exactly what was on Su-Lee's mind.

"Why not just transform and swim back that way? We'll be out here all day if we're scrambling to find a boat or Jet Ski to take us home."

"I agree," Tonia said. She needed the distraction anyhow. The thought of swimming with the other orcas, letting the water rush through her, was more than a welcoming experience for her. "We haven't turned into our alter egos for a while. Besides, I need the distraction."

"So do I." Su-Lee started stripping out of her clothes. "Let's do it. The sooner we can get out of here, the better."

"All right! A peep show! I'll go tell the others," Stin said. Stin raced back to the house. Su-Lee shook her head.

"Boy, I tell you about men—" She turned and saw Tonia had disappeared. Her eyes roamed from the house back to the ocean. "Tonia?" Relief flooded through her when she heard a splash coming from the ocean. Su-Lee took off the rest of her clothes and dived headfirst into the water. It didn't take her long to find Tonia swimming back to the island. Su-Lee picked up the pace and joined her friend as they swam out to the ocean and back toward the place that gave them solace…

***

Mandy stepped out onto the cold snow. Her feet landed on the powdery substance until she got close to the ocean. Mandy was grateful Su-Lee and Tonia had dived into the water before her. If Lex and Stin hadn't convinced her to go to a party at the bar and grill to celebrate Lex and her being official members of the Truson S.E.T., then she knew Su-Lee and Tonia would have convinced her of the same thing. She admitted to being happy about the occasion at first, but her attitude turned sour when Tonia announced her feelings for Ford to everyone in the room.

And here she thought Tonia had finally let go of her stupid crush…

But what if it's not a crush? Ford didn't reject her…

"Shut up!" she said. She kicked the snow with her shoe and sent it into the water.

The snow shined with shades of blue, sparkling with the electricity she gave out before it sank into the ocean. Why should she have cared whether Tonia wanted him or not? It was apparent Ford didn't care about her. He couldn't even admit his true feelings for her.

You can't admit your true feelings either.

Mandy growled. Her inner critic was right. How could she have possibly been so stupid as to think that a man like Vernon could truly love her? She was so hell-bent on making her parents happy by marrying him, she had risked her own safety and happiness, which almost cost her life…

Thank God she remembered what happened before she lost her life *again.*

The whole time Ford tried to warn her about her own husband. He did everything he possibly could to protect her, and she wouldn't listen to reason. Now Tonia had expressed her love and devotion to Ford, and Ford didn't object to it.

Now you've probably lost him forever, all because of your love and devotion to a man who turned out to be your worst nightmare.

"Mandy?" She shut her eyes when his voice rang in the air. She didn't want to hear the horrible rejection.

She stared into his brown eyes and waited.

CHAPTER SEVENTEEN

Silence fell between them while they stared. Mandy waited for him to say something…anything to fill the emptiness inside her stomach. If he was going to break her heart, the least he could do was say something.

"Mandy, I need to talk to you. I really need—"

"You don't have to explain yourself Ford. You were only supposed to help me until you knew the truth about what happened…"

"And until the training was over. From the way you hit that huge piece of ice, you still have a lot of training to do," Ford said.

"I don't think I do and whatever training I need, I'm pretty sure Stin will teach me." A small laugh escaped Ford. As much as she wanted to hate his laughter, she couldn't. She couldn't remember the last time she heard him laugh. She had to admit it sent tingles down her spine.

"What's so funny?" she asked.

"No offense but Stin will have a lot on his plate. I don't plan on returning to teach right away unless—" Ford stepped closer and brushed his fingers against her cheek. "—I start teaching one-on-one with you" A wave of desire flooded through her. Teach one-on-one? She didn't think she could be in the same room with him after he just declared his love and undying devotion to another woman. A woman who tried to kill her twice. She drew her face away from him and started walking in the other direction.

"You know what? You don't get to do this to me. You don't get to butter me up so you can be close to me and then toss me away like I mean nothing to you." Ford squinted and cocked his head to the side.

"What are you talking about?" he asked.

Mandy could tell he was confused. *Do I really need to spell it out for him?*

"I know you agreed to be with Tonia, okay? I'm not stupid, and I would really appreciate it if you didn't insult my intelligence by lying to me about it." She waited.

Ford shook his head.

"Mandy, I turned down her proposal. Tonia's a great friend, but I don't think it would work out between us— especially after what she did to you." Ford strolled over to her, and Mandy took a step back causing Ford to stop dead in his tracks. "Mandy, you have no idea how the last few days have been for me. I never thought I would be able to feel the way I feel for you."

Mandy swallowed. Was this an act? Clearly, he wasn't saying what she thought he was going to say.

It's not like he loves you the way you love him.

The revelation took her by surprise. Love? That was impossible. How could she possibly love someone she'd only known for a couple of days?

"Mandy, when I realized I had feelings for you, I tried to push them away as much as possible. I figured there was no way I could ever love someone else the way I loved Roxanne." Mandy's weight shifted. She twiddled her thumbs to avoid looking at him.

"So, what does that mean for us? Where do we stand, Ford?" *Do you see a future for us?* The last thought she had shifted through her mind again. She wanted to be wrong on so many levels, but she knew she wasn't. Her mind kept replaying the words until she couldn't hear herself think. The more she repeated them, the more she couldn't deny it.

She was in love with Ford Mayfield.

He stroked her hands. Heat surged through her. Her alter ego jumped at his touch. She welcomed the invitation to do much more.

"Mandy, I don't know what our future holds for either of us. All I know is that I'm in love with you. When I first saw you, I shut myself off because of my love for my wife." He paused. "But over these last couple of days, my feelings for you have grown.

"When I heard you left, I went searching for you. Then to hear you were kidnapped by the Transforments—I almost lost my mind. The thought of losing you was more than I could bear. I knew you were out there alone with Lex and—" He exhaled. "I really wished you hadn't disappeared."

"I needed to protect you. My powers were too strong. I thought I had almost killed you. I couldn't stand there and watch you suffer."

"But I lived. I fought to come back to you Mandy. I dreamed of a life with you and you know what? I enjoyed it. I didn't want it to end."

"Hey Ford! We have to go man. Su-Lee and Tonia already beat us back to the island. We need to head back," Stin said, his word echoing through the night sky. *Perfect getaway,* Mandy thought. Though he was saying all the right things, Mandy didn't want to stick around and believe his story, no matter how good it sounded at the moment.

The air had turned cooler than before, and she really wanted to get inside a nice cozy bed and relax. After today's events, all she wanted to do was to go to sleep and forget this nightmare she once called a life…and maybe forget or at least sort out the feelings she had in her head.

"Wait up Stin, I'm coming!" Mandy started jogging toward Stin but stopped when Ford grabbed her arm.

"Mandy wait, I really need to say this." The contact brought back memories of her and Vernon's history, causing her to jerk her arm away from him.

"Ford, it's been a long night. I'm tired. All I want to do is go to sleep. I appreciate everything you said, but I think we should just leave everything the way it is until tomorrow."

"But Mandy I—"

"Good night, Ford." Mandy jogged toward Stin and the others as they headed into the ocean. After a couple of jogs, Mandy stripped naked and dived into the water. Relief flooded through her when the water massaged her skin. She wanted to ignore the feelings she felt for Ford and move on, especially after her ordeal with Vernon. Maybe she wasn't ready for this type of relationship…

Mandy blocked out her emotions again. *All of this can wait until tomorrow. Don't think about it tonight.* And she remained silent until she made it to the island.

***

Mandy, I love you.

Those were the words Ford wanted to say to her. For a moment, he thought he finally got to her, that she saw what he felt all along and thought she felt the same way he did. It was when the conversation had turned in a different direction that he realized it wasn't going the way he expected. His heart sank. Did she not believe the words he spoke? He tried to think of a way to convince her he wanted her to stay with him and no one else.

His mind reflected back to the conversation Stin and he had about Mandy. He didn't want her to feel like she was just a one-night stand. But how could he prove it? During the time they were together, he never knew what she liked, what she didn't like…he was too busy trying to focus on ignoring his feelings for her, telling himself there was no way he could feel the way he felt for her.

That was a huge mistake on his part.

"Ford?" His eyes shifted to Su-Lee and her naked body. He tore his eyes away from her by focusing on her face. "Ford? Are you okay?"

"Yeah, I'm fine," he said. He reached for his pockets but couldn't find them. He looked at himself. He was naked too. "Did I transform already?"

Su-Lee nodded. "You don't remember?"

Ford cleared his throat.

"No, I don't." He searched the island for his cabin. When he found the small blue light on his door, he knew he'd found his home. "I don't even remember transitioning."

"Whoa, she really has you hooked, huh?" Su-Lee asked.

He opened his mouth to protest, but Su-Lee was already walking toward Nise's. Ford raced back to his cabin despite the onlookers staring at him in the middle of night. He grabbed the first pair of clothes he saw in his closet and shoved them on, thinking about how he could approach Mandy. He wanted to take her someplace special where there were no interruptions. He needed to tell her how he felt without Stin whispering in his ear how much easier it would be to nail her and walk away.

He just wanted *her*.

Once dressed, he opened the door. It was another cool night but without a snowstorm. Still, with all the severe storms raging for the last couple of days, the snow had piled up to at least eighteen feet deep. Ford focused his attention on the nice elderly couple standing a few feet away from the spectacular light exhibit invading the night sky.

The woman turned to the man sitting next to her.

"Isn't it beautiful George? Why I've never seen anything so gorgeous in all my years of being on this earth."

"Yeah, it's also very dangerous." The man grunted. A rainbow of colors glistened and shimmered throughout the whole shore of the island. The colors glowed so brightly, Ford could see them for miles.

The Northern Lights.

He remembered how much he wanted to just sit and relax in a chair with Roxanne and watch how the lights danced and interacted with each other, but Roxanne thought it was boring. *I would rather sit and watch it on TV than sit out in the cold and watch it from the other side of town.*

Ford never brought it up again after that.

But now he might have the possibility to share it with someone he desperately needed in his life. He didn't care if she brought Lex along with her—as far as he was concerned, Lex was part of the family as well.

His family.

It was time for him to stop hiding how he felt and tell her what he truly wanted…

***

"Can I have a double shot of tequila please?" Mandy shot out from across the room and watched the owner put her hands on her hips in return. What was her damn problem? All she asked was for two shots of tequila, not a whole pint. Mandy leaned her head forward and scoffed.

She didn't know what Stin was talking about when he said Nise's Bar and Grill was the best.

Clearly it wasn't the case for her.

Wasn't she supposed to be the newest member of the group? Wasn't she supposed to be treated like royalty? What the hell happened to customer service?

"Whoa, you really need to calm down girl." Mandy turned and faced Su-Lee who sat next to her.

"I'm sorry, I was having a private conversation with myself. I don't think anyone else was invited," Mandy said. Nise slammed the two glasses on the table, and one of the drinks spilled over onto the smooth and colorful tile in front of them.

"Look girl, I don't know who you are or what your problem is, but if you don't take that attitude and shove it, I'll have you banned from this bar, got it?" Mandy jumped from the table. She tried to grab Nise's shirt and remind her who she was talking to, but Su-Lee touched her arm before the action took place.

"I'm sorry Nise. I'm afraid my new friend here had a little too much to drink. I'll handle this while you focus on the other customers, okay?" Su-Lee said and winked.

"You better." Nise grabbed a black tray and arranged all of the alcohol before lifting it with one hand and strutting away to her next customers. Mandy snatched her arm away.

"I didn't need you to defend me back there. I could have handled it myself!"

Su-Lee shook her head.

"Seriously Mandy, what's with the attitude? I thought you would be grateful to be here. If you're not then you should be. Do you know how much of an honor it is to be a member of this team?" Mandy downed two glasses of tequila, letting the sensation burn the back of her throat. She welcomed the feeling it gave her—serving as a punishment for falling in love with someone she hardly knew.

How could she be so stupid?

The worst part about the whole situation was her running back to someone who ended up being a murderer. She couldn't even comprehend how someone like Ford who was strong and brave to the core of his being could ever fall in love with someone who was so naive and dumb?

He deserved better.

"Mandy, did you hear me?" Mandy took a deep breath.

"I heard you loud and clear Su-Lee. Don't get me wrong, I'm grateful to be a part of the team, it's just—" Mandy stopped mid-sentence. She twirled the glass with her hand until a shadow loomed over both of them.

"Excuse me girls. I don't mean to interrupt, but could I have a moment alone with Mandy? There's something I would really like to say," the familiar voice said. It didn't take Mandy long to figure out who the voice belonged to. She couldn't face another rejection from him. She needed her space.

"Sure." Su-Lee got up from the chair and laid a hand on Mandy's shoulder. "Just hear him out Mandy. I think he may surprise you." Su-Lee patted her shoulder and strutted back to the rest of the group.

"Look, I don't want to hear what you have to say, okay? I've made up my mind. I'm staying with Stin—Lex and I are staying with Stin and that's the end of it." Mandy pounded her fist on the table. They stared at each other before Ford leaned over and kissed her. Blood rushed through her veins. She felt the electricity vibrate through her skin. Her alter ego agreed with the kiss wholeheartedly. She was fighting to get out and mate with the only person she ever loved.

She didn't want to stop.

Ford must have read her mind as he pressed his body against hers. Heat surged through them. Mandy felt Ford's hands roam around her back. Her breasts pressed against his chest, a sensation that went through Ford's spine like fire in his body.

Ford jerked away, ending the kiss abruptly.

"I'm sorry, that wasn't—" Ford stopped himself before starting again. "There's something I would like to show you, I think you would really enjoy it."

Show me? She didn't know what to expect when it came to what he wanted to show her, but this time she couldn't resist the offer or him. "Ok," she said. A smile formed across Ford's lips. Mandy felt his hand on her back as he ushered her toward the door.

"Wait, where are you going? We were going to swear Lex and Mandy in as the newest member of the team, you can't leave now," Stin said.

"We'll be back. Mandy and I have to talk about something first." Ford opened the door and let Mandy walk through while Stin threw his hands in the air.

"Well hurry up. If I keep the members here any longer, they're not going to remember the ceremony," Stin said. Mandy stepped out onto the snow, the cold snapping her out of the lust-filled desire she had for Ford.

"What is this about? What is it that you have to show me?" Mandy watched Ford stare up into the night sky before focusing on her.

"Come here." He gently pulled on her arm and pointed. "You see that?"

Mandy turned. A huge ray of green fluorescent lights glowed in the distance. Tiny stars and dust accompanied the light, making it look like the stars were coming down to Earth and settling onto the ground. She smiled.

"How is it doing that? I've never seen anything like it before."

"You like it?" Ford asked.

"I love it. It's the most beautiful thing I've ever seen." Silence crept between them as Mandy stared at the lights. There was a rainbow of color and shapes, each one more vibrant than the next.

"It's funny. After ten years of being married to Roxanne, I never dreamed it was possible to have feelings for another woman." Ford paused. After she died, I thought there was no way I could possibly move on, but I have. The same way you feel about those lights is how I feel about you."

Mandy's heart pounded her chest. What was he saying? She hoped it was everything she had been feeling for the last couple of days she'd been on the island. Ford inched closer to her.

"Mandy, I don't know what's going to happen between us. I don't know if we're going to get married and have children. I don't know if we're going to be soul mates for the rest of our lives. Hell, I don't even know if we're going to be together six months down the road." He paused and took her hand. The contact made every organ in her body quiver.

"All I know is that I can't deny the feelings I have for you. I thought I was never going to feel the same way about any other woman after my wife's death, but that's not the case anymore. I can finally say that I'm in love again."

Mandy's heart soared. *He just said he was in love with me!* She couldn't believe her ears. The moment she stared into his eyes, she knew what he said and felt were real. There was no doubt she felt the same way he did.

"Oh Ford, I'm in love with you too." She wiped away the moisture streaming from her eyes. "I didn't want to believe it either, especially after I found out about the marriage I had with Vernon. I felt so guilty about hurting you that I felt I had no other choice but to walk away."

"I know you would never intentionally hurt me Mandy. I went searching for you the moment I woke up." He paused. "Mandy, the mere thought of you getting hurt or killed by Vernon or any of his army would have killed me. He might as well have taken me too." He leaned closer, his hot breath massaging Mandy's skin. Her alter ego wanted to be in Ford's company this very moment, but she pushed her away.

Ford kissed her again, this time harder and faster than ever before. His tongue ripped through every sensation in her skin. The smell of his scent mixed in with the cool ocean breeze in the night sky gave a shift of sexual energy she'd never experienced before. She continued the tango with him, their tongues stimulating enough body heat to light up a fire. When Ford managed to pull away all of her clothes and set them aside on the shore, she gave no objection.

His hands smoothed over her body. He cupped her breasts and flicked his tongue on her nipples, licking and sucking them until Mandy screamed out his name, the sound echoing throughout the night.

So sweet. So warm. So inviting…

How could she have survived this long without this wonderful feeling?

Stop thinking about the past. Focus on him.

She lifted her weight to give him access to her nipples, sucking on one then the other until she felt the tension building inside her. A fluttering sensation formed in her gut. She was close. She could feel it burning.

He stopped.

Mandy lay back and waited. Was that all? Was that all he wanted to do? The questions stopped once Ford left a trail of kisses down her tummy. He carefully pried her legs open and buried his face, sopping up the moisture etched between her thighs. Mandy gently stroked the curly blond strands of his hair while he massaged her slick folds.

"Can't hold it…anymore…feel it…coming…" Mandy said through clenched teeth. She gazed at Ford and the bulge inside his pants. She grabbed onto him and wrestled with his pants until the bulge was free. Desire swept through her. Ford didn't hesitate to put his hands on her hips and with a gentle thrust, weep deep inside her. Sensations of her expanding her body to meet his length was enough for her to shiver. Another thrust, this time harder than the first, made her grasp.

"Too much?" he asked. His brow lifted. Was he challenging her? Or was it just her imagining things?

"No, want more. Give me all of you, Ford." With that command, Ford thrust himself inside her. The aching she felt for this man was finally satisfied. Mandy felt herself losing control as she inched closer to her climax…

He shouted. She felt his release, the liquid pouring into her core. A moment later, she felt her release as well. It was enough to make Ford collapse on top of her. She welcomed him by wrapping her arms around him.

Her alter ego screamed with glee and satisfaction before calming. Either way, she enjoyed him being in her arms, embracing every scent swimming through her nostrils. This was going to be marked as one of the greatest experiences in her life. She couldn't remember the last time sex had felt so good.

"Are you all right?" Ford asked as he carefully sat up on the bed. Mandy smiled and snuggled next to him, her head leaning against his shoulder.

"I'm better than I've ever been," Mandy said. She meant every word of it. Who cared if she didn't like the cold? A girl could get used to the chilly temperatures as long as she was able to hold on to this wonderful man every night for the rest of their lives. She stared into Ford's brown eyes, and her body tingled when he smiled.

"I'm glad. I thought I was going to hurt you for a second," he said. He snuggled his nose against her neck. "Are you ready for the ceremony now?"

The ceremony at Nise's Bar and Grill. Mandy snapped her head back. She had completely forgotten about it. She remembered how rude she was to Nise. She owed her a huge apology for the way she acted. On top of everything else, the rest of the team was waiting on them to swear both her and Lex in as the new members of the Truson Super Elite Team. Stin seemed happy about the whole event. She couldn't let him down.

"As long as I'm with you, I can handle it."

"In that case—" he stood. "We need to get ready quickly or else Stin won't be too happy, and I know I don't want him moping about it for the next two months." He paused and extended his hand. "Shall we?"

"I'll be able to go as soon as we get dressed. Can't walk into a bar naked. Think of the attention we'd get," Mandy said.

Ford laughed. "You're right. I think we should get dressed first."

"That sounds like a plan."

CHAPTER EIGHTEEN

Ford wasn't expecting the plans to change. He was under the impression the members were only going to swear in Mandy and Lex and then celebrate until everyone got tired and went home. That was the typical celebration at Nise's Bar and Grill. Dr. Madison would read the rules from the Book of Truson, the newest member would recite the rules and would promise to live by them until the end of time, everyone would clap and then give the latest member either a hug or a slap on the back welcoming him or her into the group.

This time was different.

Based on Tonia's suggestion and the fact that Dr. Madison's body was decomposing in the box, the rest of the members decided to hold a ceremony for her sudden death. Ford hated they made the decision without including him, but he knew they were only doing what was best for Dr. Madison and the team. It was her and her family that carried the tradition of the team, it was only natural they would want to celebrate her death…

He just hadn't wanted it to be this soon…

"I know that tonight was supposed to be one of celebration, one in which we swore and accepted two of the newest members into our team and into our world." Stin took a moment to observe the room before he continued.

"But today, I also want to honor the woman who has carried on the tradition of the Truson Super Elite Team for generations. Even though she was very used to scraping on our last nerves whenever she had a problem or better yet, when Dr. Madison wanted to test out her latest experiment with the Animan Three-Hundred, she was always there for us whenever we needed her."

Ford nodded but remained silent. He snuck a glance at Mandy to see if she was okay. Her face remained sullen. She didn't even look his way while Stin continued with the speech.

"Tonight, I won't spend too much time talking about her considering there is another ceremony that will be taking place. But before we give one last goodbye to the woman who created the last generation of Ormans, I wanted to raise my glass—" Stin lifted his glass from the table and extended it to the sky. "—to the woman who gave us a second chance at love and life. Here's to you Dr. Madison, may you rest in peace."

"Here, here." Everyone raised their glass and took a swig. Ford gave out a sly grin and searched around to see if Nise was offering anything to toast with.

"You know I couldn't leave my favorite member out in the cold to toast his favorite girl," Nise said.

Ford and Mandy turned.

"Hello Nise, how's everything going?" Ford asked. He took the glass from the tray and swallowed the contents. Mandy took a couple of sips before she made eye contact with the woman. Nise focused her attention on Ford again.

"So, how are you feeling? Are you okay with everything?"

"Now I am." He set the glass on the tray. "Thank you."

"You're welcome. I guess I'll be going then."

"Wait!" Mandy said. Nise turned.

"I just wanted to let you know how sorry I am for the way I acted. I was upset about something, and I shouldn't have taken it out on you."

"Let me guess, you thought Ford was interested in that brown-haired woman—Tonia, right?"

"Tread carefully Nise," Ford warned. "And how did you know about that anyway?" Nise shrugged.

"Don't you know word gets around on this island? After being here for a decade, I got to know all of you and your craziness." Nise paused and focused her attention on Mandy. "You shouldn't have to worry though. I knew the moment I saw him waking up on the island butt-naked without any sense of how he got here, something was wrong."

"Nise!" Ford barked. Both of them turned at the sound of laughter echoing the room.

"And why are you laughing Su-Lee? What seems to be so funny?" Mandy asked. It wasn't bad enough that

Nise saw her man naked on the island, now Su-Lee was laughing about something she didn't find funny at all.

"Because it's the truth, Ford." Su-Lee shrugged her shoulders. "C'mon Ford, I've seen you naked before. Half of the team has seen you naked before. You shouldn't worry about it too much Mandy. We know he only has eyes for you."

Ford gripped Mandy's hand so hard, she could hear the bones starting to crack in her skin. Luckily, Mandy didn't have to tell him he was hurting her for him to pay attention. Ford immediately loosened his grip. She felt the heat of his hand lessen as he carefully let go and tried to control himself.

"I'm glad you clarified this. I'm hoping next time, it won't happen again, and you two will at least try to control yourselves whenever you see him naked," Mandy said. She turned to Nise. "Again, I apologize for my rude behavior. All I ask is that you deliver on my request." Nise shrugged.

"Apology accepted. You probably had a lot to deal with concerning your new life and everything. I hope it works out well for you and I will honor your request."

"Thank you." Mandy smiled. Nise smiled back and raised her tray.

"More alcohol for the celebration?"

Both Mandy and Ford shook their heads, no. Ford could feel the tension rising in his throat when Stin and the others gathered around him. This was going to be the hardest part—the burial.

"Are you sure Dr. Madison wanted her body floating in the ice-cold water? The snow is frozen. How are we going to give her a proper burial?" Su-Lee asked.

"I think it would be better if her body was burned so we could spread her ashes over the ocean," Gabriel piped in. Ford saw the other members nod in agreement. Which meant he had to set her on fire to fulfill the request—something he didn't look forward to.

Focus on the task. You can do this.

Stin, Tonia, and Mandy grabbed the coffin and carefully laid Dr. Madison's body on the ground.

"Does anyone have an urn for her ashes?" Stin asked. The team stared at each other until Mandy raised and wiggled her finger.

"I'll be right back," she said. She blazed through the snow and ran inside the bar.

"Where the hell do she think she's going?" Tonia barked. "How can you guys just let her take off like that?"

"Tonia, I love you to death, but I think you need to cut it out right now," Su-Lee responded. Tonia scoffed.

"What is she holding?" Stin asked. Everyone focused their attention on Mandy as she ran out of Nise's Bar and Grill with a flower pot in her hands.

"This was the best thing I could find," she said.

"It will work." Ford took the pot. "Who is going to do the honors?" Tonia raised her hand.

"I'll do it." Ford passed the flower pot to Tonia while the rest grabbed a glass and raised it in the air.

"To Dr. Madison who brought us all together and made sure we were the best team on the planet. Cheers!" The team all raised their glasses in the air.

"To Dr. Madison," Stin said as he downed his drink. The team downed their drinks as well before making their way to the ocean.

I'm the leader. This is what a leader does, leads his team no matter what.

So why the hell did he feel so guilty about burying her here? Why did he feel so responsible for her death? As Tonia poured the ashes into the water, the mere thought of her nonexistence made him want to punch a wall. Why did this have to happen? He should have paid more attention to her, should have followed her and told her she needed to stay where she was and finish what they had discovered together. Hell, maybe he should have just demanded she remained on the island for her protection.

"She would have put up a fight, you know that."

Ford sighed. There were times when Ford would have been alone than deal with anyone giving him advice on how to grieve when it came to the people he cared about. He remembered how much he tore his team apart after Roxanne died. He shut everyone out and continued to drink and have sex with all sorts of women to ease the pain.

Not today. Not anymore.

He welcomed any advice Mandy wanted to give him to deal with the emotions he'd been experiencing within the last few days.

"You shouldn't be so hard on yourself. She would have demanded to go," Mandy said. Her soothing voice seemed to calm down his alter ego, but it did very little to his emotions.

"I shouldn't have been such a jerk to her. I should have—" Before he could utter another word, her finger landed on his lips.

"I won't let you do it, Ford Mayfield. I won't let you go through this pity party again." She cradled his face. "This was not your fault. I'm pretty sure if you commanded her to stay, she would have fought you tooth and nail on it." Ford let her comment sink in. She was right. He needed to stop blaming himself for what happened. He needed to move on.

"And now for the happiest occasion of all. Mandy and Lex's declaration of being the two newest members of our team. Ford?" Ford stared directly at Stin and waited.

"Would you like to do the honors?"

Ford's eyes darted to Mandy. Mandy smiled and held onto Ford's hand as they carefully walked in front of the group. Lex wasn't too far behind, and he stood right next to Ford, waiting for what was going to happen.

"Su-Lee, the book please." Su-Lee stepped forward with the thick ebony bound manual in her hand and gave it to Ford. Ford and Su-Lee exchanged smiles before she managed to sit back down. Ford flipped through the first couple of pages until he landed on the Three Rules of Truson. He cleared his throat.

"Let's get this ceremony over with," he said. "Lex, come stand next to Mandy please." Lex walked up to

Mandy and held her hand. Ford wasted little time reciting the rules.

"Rule #1: One must respect and value our ancestors. They are here to offer spiritual guidance and advice, and it is up to us to respect them."

"Rule #2: One must never do harm to another member of the Truson Super Elite Team unless it's absolutely necessary. We must honor and respect one another as a family, not as enemies."

Ford paused once he got to rule #3. Even though it was written in the book before his time, Dr. Madison always enforced the rule—a rule he thought was a little unfair. How was he supposed to know he would fall in love with one of the newest members of the Truson Super Elite Team? The rules were sometimes a little difficult to follow, especially when it came to these types of situations.

What was he to do?

Dr. Madison is gone. Have to change the rules.

"This final rule I think I will change because I've always thought it a little unorthodox." Mandy and Lex turned to each other before they decided to focus on Ford again.

"Rule #3 states that one must never fall in love with any member of the Truson Super Elite Team whatsoever." Ford paused. "I don't know why this rule is in here, but as of today, I'm officially changing it. As of this very moment, Rule #3 is off the table."

Huge applause erupted from the crowd before Ford lifted his hand to get their attention again.

"We are ready to begin." Ford's eyes darted to Mandy. "Mandy, you're up first." Mandy put her hand on the book.

"Repeat after me: I solemnly swear—"

"I solemnly swear."

"To uphold and obey these rules…"

"As the newest member of the Truson Super Elite Team," Ford finished.

"As the newest member of the Truson Super Elite Team."

Ford smiled. He faced the crowd.

"Ladies and gentlemen, may I present to you the newest female member of the Truson S.E.T." Another round of applause. Ford decided to make the night more interesting by pulling her close and giving her a kiss. The crowd cheered louder. Ford carefully let go and turned to Lex.

"Are you ready?"

Lex gave out a small grin and nodded.

"I'll be out of your way then," Mandy said. She stepped down and motioned Lex to come forward. Ford repeated the same rules again to Lex. Lex agreed to the terms and another roar of the crowd echoed throughout the sky. It was a glorious feeling Ford wouldn't soon forget.

After the ceremony, Ford, Mandy, Lex and the rest of the crew decided to spend the evening at Nise's Bar and Grill. Ford and Mandy watched as Lex and Stin held their own private conversation in one corner while Su-Lee and Tonia chatted away in another.

"How come they were able to bring you back to life and not Roxanne?" Mandy asked. Nise laid another drink on the table. Ford took a swig before he answered.

"Roxanne never came back after the Animan was injected into her system. The doctors tried to bring her back, but—" Ford shook his head. He felt her hand massage his shoulder.

"I'm so sorry."

"We had so many plans for the future…she wanted us to have a baby once we returned from our trip. We were about to renew our vows and everything." Ford avoided looking at Mandy as his eyes roamed the bar.

"There were days where I wished I could go back and fix what happened. All I wanted was to get back to the life we shared. I felt like I was losing her in some way because of the attention Vernon was giving her. I became too busy in my own life and didn't see what was going on in front of me. She needed my attention. She wanted us to go back to the way we were." He cleared his throat. "It's too bad I didn't pay attention sooner."

Ford grabbed both of Mandy's hands.

"But all that is in the past. The most important thing to me at this moment is you. For a whole decade, I thought I would never fall in love again. I used to be just like Stin—get drunk, sleep with all sorts of women, not caring about who they were as long as I got what I wanted in the end."

Mandy nodded.

"I must say you don't strike me as being like Stin. You seem to be a loner most of the time. For a moment, I thought you didn't have any friends." Ford and Mandy both shared a laugh.

"These members are my friends. It's not that I don't enjoy being with them sometimes, I just prefer to be alone with my thoughts," Ford said. The smile faded. "Now that my past is fading, I wanted to say something before we celebrate the night away." Mandy's heart pounded in her chest. What else could he possibly say? So far, she was enjoying his company and the words he spoke. *Please, don't ruin this. Don't say what I think you're gonna say.*

"Yes, Ford?"

"I wanted you to know that even though Roxanne will always have a special place in my heart, you do too and despite the ups and downs we went through within these last couple of days, I never stopped loving you, and I honestly think I never will." Ford inched closer. "If I do, then that would be the perfect time to use your powers to kill me."

Mandy leaned in close to him. "I will and by the way, I love you too Ford Mayfield."

"Let's say you and I skip the celebration and make another go at my cabin?" Ford asked. Mandy turned back to the party and shrugged.

"Let's do it."

As Ford and Mandy strolled out of the bar and into the cold night, all Mandy wanted was to relive this night and many more nights with him forever…

Author Bio

Dominique Gibson knew she wanted to be a writer ever since she sat down at her plastic table and started writing stories out of sheer boredom at eight-years-old. Several years later, she decided to pursue a bachelor's degree in Fiction Writing from Columbia College Chicago. After pursuing a degree in Early Childhood Administration to support her career in Early Childhood Education, Dominique decided to go back and pursue a degree she always wanted: An MFA in creative writing. To learn more about her and her books, please visit her website at dominiquegibsonauthor.com, Dominique Gibson on Facebook, and @dominq79453763 on Twitter.

www.ingramcontent.com/pod-product-compliance
Lightning Source LLC
Chambersburg PA
CBHW060707190726
48289CB00002B/576